Rudyard Kipling (1865–1936) was born in Bombay, the son of an Anglo-Indian professor of architectural sculpture. There he was brought up in the care of "ayahs," or native nurses, who taught him Hindustani and the native lore that haunted his imagination. At the age of six, he was sent to school in England at Westward Ho!, the setting for *Stalky & Co.* In 1883, he returned to India and embarked on a career in journalism, writing the news stories as well as the tales and ballads that began to make his reputation. After seven years, he went back to England, the literary star of the hour. He married an American and settled down in Vermont from 1892 to 1894. Then he returned to the English countryside, where he remained, except for a few trips abroad, for the rest of his life. The author of innumerable stories and poems, Rudyard Kipling is especially known for *Soldiers Three* (1888), *The Light That Failed* (1890), *The Jungle Books* (1894–95), *Captains Courageous* (1897), *Stalky & Co.* (1899), *Kim* (1901), and *Just So Stories* (1902). Among many other honors, he received the Nobel Prize for Literature in 1907.

Educated at Oxford University, where he read modern history, **Andrew Lycett** is an author and journalist who has lived and worked on the Indian subcontinent. His books include biographies of Rudyard Kipling and Ian Fleming, and he is currently working on a life of the poet Dylan Thomas.

RUDYARD
KIPLING

BARRACK-ROOM
BALLADS

With a New Introduction and
Annotations by Andrew Lycett

A SIGNET CLASSIC

SIGNET CLASSIC
Published by New American Library, a division of
Penguin Group (USA) Inc., 375 Hudson Street,
New York, New York 10014, U.S.A.
Penguin Books Ltd, 80 Strand,
London WC2R 0RL, England
Penguin Books Australia Ltd, 250 Camberwell Road,
Camberwell, Victoria 3124, Australia
Penguin Books Canada Ltd, 10 Alcorn Avenue,
Toronto, Ontario, Canada M4V 3B2
Penguin Books (N.Z.) Ltd, Cnr Rosedale and Airborne Roads,
Albany, Auckland 1310, New Zealand

Penguin Books Ltd, Registered Offices:
80 Strand, London WC2R 0RL, England

Published by Signet Classic, an imprint of New American Library,
a division of Penguin Group (USA) Inc.

First Signet Classic Printing, June 2003
10 9 8 7 6 5 4 3 2 1

Introduction and notes copyright © Andrew Lycett, 2003
All rights reserved

 REGISTERED TRADEMARK—MARCA REGISTRADA

Library of Congress Catalog Card Number: 2002037857

Printed in the United States of America

CONTENTS

Introduction　　vii

To T. A.　　*3*

Danny Deever　　*4*

Tommy　　*7*

"Fuzzy-Wuzzy"　　*10*

Soldier, Soldier　　*13*

Screw-Guns　　*15*

Cells　　*18*

Gunga Din　　*20*

Oonts　　*23*

Loot　　*26*

"Snarleyow"　　*29*

The Widow at Windsor　　*32*

Belts　　*34*

The Young British Soldier　　*37*

Mandalay　　*40*

Troopin'　　*43*

The Widow's Party　　*45*

Ford o' Kabul River　　*47*

Gentlemen-Rankers　　*49*

Route Marchin'　　*52*

Shillin' a Day　　*55*

Prelude　　*57*

v

Contents

"Back to the Army Again" 58

"Birds of Prey" March 62

"Soldier an' Sailor Too" 65

Sappers 68

That Day 71

"The Men That Fought at Minden" 74

Cholera Camp 77

The Ladies 80

Bill 'Awkins 83

The Mother-Lodge 84

"Follow Me 'Ome" 87

The Sergeant's Weddin' 89

The Jacket 91

The 'Eathen 94

The Shut-Eye Sentry 99

"Mary, Pity Women!" 102

For to Admire 104

L'envoi 106

Selected Bibliography 107

INTRODUCTION

From the Peloponnesian War to the Gulf War, music and songs have been essential features of a soldier's world. Bugle calls, regimental marches, hymns, bawdy limericks and plaintive laments: whether in the heat of battle or the hierarchical world of the barracks, these provide simple, direct means of communication to maintain discipline, boost morale or simply let off steam—in fact, to cope with all the stresses and strains of army life.

The British writer Rudyard Kipling recognized the powerful effect of song and incorporated its emotion, rhythm and sense of camaraderie into his *Barrack-Room Ballads,* the series of poems he wrote in the 1890s about the experience of military service in India and other parts of the British Empire.

Kipling was a complicated, brilliant man who wrote many things well—not just poems, but stories, novels and journalism. Not for nothing was he awarded the Nobel Prize for Literature in 1907. He was born in Bombay (now Mumbai) in December 1865, the son of a teacher at the local art college and a spirited Irish-Scottish woman who was related to the well-known Pre-Raphaelite painter Edward Burne-Jones.

At the age of five, Kipling was sent back to England to live with foster parents (an experience he loathed) and later to attend the United Services College, a school for officers who fought in often forgotten campaigns in all corners of the Empire.

Since young Kipling's aptitude was for literature rather than for battle, he returned to India at the age of sixteen and joined the staff of the daily newspaper, the *Civil and Military Gazette* in Lahore, the Punjab town where his parents had moved, after his father, Lockwood, was appointed keeper of the local museum.

Kipling slowly readjusted to living in colonial India. Initially he stuck to journalism, demonstrating his sharp eye for color and detail in his reports on corruption in municipal politics in Lahore or the decadence of princely courts. As he traveled more widely, he began to satirize the manipulativeness, self-interest and crass stupidity of his fellow "Anglo-Indians" in a series of poems he called *Departmental Ditties* and in his stories known as *Plain Tales from the Hills*.

At the same time, he grew to understand the nature of Empire. Despite his general cynicism, he came genuinely to admire the self-sacrifice of doctors, engineers and other administrators who devoted their lives to bringing sanitation, roads and other benefits of Western civilization to remote areas of India. He convinced himself this was a noble cause. As was clear throughout his life, the doers of Empire became his heroes.

Another body was also essential to getting things done in imperial India: the military. Five miles east of Lahore stood the Mian Mir military cantonment, where an infantry battalion and artillery battery were always stationed. Kipling frequently rode over to Mian Mir, where he made it his business to meet not only the officers in their messes but also the enlisted men in their dusty quarters.

Greatly admiring the humor and fortitude of the ordinary soldier in often appalling conditions, he embarked on a series of stories about their life in India. These tales, as collected in *Soldiers Three*, featured a trio of enlisted men: the Irishman Terence Mulvaney, the Cockney Stanley Ortheris and the Yorkshire-born Jock Learoyd. No one had previously given fictional voice in this way to lowly privates such as Mulvaney, who in "With the Main Guard" asks, "Mary, Mother av Mercy, fwat the divil possist us to take an' kape this melancholious counthry? Answer me that, sorr."

Kipling took up the causes of the rank and file in his journalism. For example, he campaigned for a more realistic approach to sex. The soldiers often used the services of local bazaar prostitutes, but the authorities made little attempt to inspect the girls involved, with the result, Kipling argued, that there were nine thousand "expensive white men a year always laid from venereal disease."

Kipling's stories appeared in six volumes of the Indian Railway Library, published by A. H. Wheeler & Co. with covers drawn by his father. Today the dialect of these soldier tales is sometimes difficult to understand. But in the late 1880s, they proved sensational. English literature was experiencing a creative lull after the vibrancy of Dickens and Thackeray. Kipling's stories provided color and energy, while introducing British readers to a hitherto unknown aspect of the expanding Empire.

One of the six volumes, *Soldiers Three,* was reviewed in the *Spectator* in London in March 1889—unusual for a book published in India. It was also well received by Sidney Low, editor of the conservative daily newspaper the *St. James's Gazette,* who pronounced enthusiastically about a new talent "who had dawned upon the eastern horizon. . . . It may be that a greater than Dickens is here." The generally positive response encouraged Kipling to give up his newspaper job and move to London to try his hand in a much more sophisticated and potentially lucrative market.

Arriving in the British capital in October 1889, Kipling immediately worried that he had made the wrong decision. Out of place among the fashionable aesthetes of the time, he wrote his well-observed poem "In Partibus," which for some reason he declined to include

in his *Collected Verse*. This chronicled his longing for
the sunshine and moral certainties of India, where the
Indian army man was

> Set up, and trimmed and taut,
> Who does not spout hashed libraries
> Or think the next man's thought,
> And walks as though he owned himself,
> And hogs his bristles short.

After a period of debilitating homesickness, Kipling
found his professional feet, especially after meeting
W. E. Henley, editor of the influential Conservative
journal the *Scots Observer*. Henley, with his wooden
leg, was the model for Long John Silver in his friend
Robert Louis Stevenson's *Treasure Island,* published
in 1883. He had been alerted to Kipling's talents by a
seafaring brother who had read one of the young
man's poems in an Indian newspaper. He invited Kip-
ling to his club, the Savile, after which his guest pro-
nounced Henley "more different varieties of man than
most"—a typically wry compliment.

Kipling agreed to work on a freelance basis for the
Scots Observer. This was not too painful: on the sur-
face, it was one of the periodicals most sympathetic
to his views. Run by a group of old-fashioned Tories
in Edinburgh, it was a forceful proponent of British
imperialism.

His first submission was a trifle—a wry Jacobean-
style meditation on love and death. However, his sec-
ond piece was "Danny Deever," a simple, graphic,
rhythmic, insistent ballad about a soldier hanged by
his regiment for shooting a colleague. When he read
it, Henley is said to have danced on his wooden leg.
Published in the *Scots Observer* on 22 February 1890,
it was immediately seized on by David Masson, the
opinion-making professor of rhetoric and English liter-
ature at Edinburgh University, who exclaimed enthusi-

astically to his students, "Here's literature! Here's literature at last!"

Kipling responded by offering Henley twelve more poems about the travails of military life, which the *Scots Observer* published over the next few months. Kipling had conceived this kind of verse while in India: in late 1888 he had offered a Calcutta publisher a volume composed of "my *Barrack-Room Ballads* and other Poems which includes 2 soldiers songs and a variety of Anglo-Indian sentimental and descriptive work," and on his journey home eastward across the Pacific Ocean and the American continent, he had hummed what he called his "Tommy Atkins ballads" to Edmonia Hill, a well-read American woman whom he had befriended in Allahabad.

However the *Barrack-Room Ballads* took real poetic form only in the particular circumstances of his life in London. As soon as he arrived, he rented a set of rooms in Villiers Street, running beside Charing Cross Station in the center of town. At the end of his street stood Gatti's, a popular music hall. Often he would go there after a day's work, four pence buying admission and a pewter jar of beer. At Gatti's he got to know something missing in India—the vibrancy of working-class culture. Inspired by the "compelling songs" of the Lion and Mammoth Comiques, he wrote to Edmonia (known as Ted) Hill, saying that London needed "a poet of the Music Halls." For his old paper, the *Civil and Military Gazette* in Lahore, he wrote a story, "My Great and Only," about a venue such as Gatti's, where, to the uninhibited accompaniment of his audience, a star belts out a ditty about a Life Guard's inexpert wooing of an undercook. Kipling composed the song himself, complete with the refrain

And that's what the Girl told the Soldier,
Soldier! Soldier!
An' that's what the Girl told the Soldier.

Such entertainments suggested to Kipling that he could bring together the immediacy of the music hall with his firsthand observations of military life (mainly gained in India). This did not mean he wanted to write music hall songs; rather, he intended to draw on popular culture for his soldier poems. And that required him to incorporate elements from the ballads, marches and laments that soldiers had written and sung through the ages, giving them a modern twist.

A ballad essentially tells a story graphically and in verse. It is rhythmic and memorable because it is hewn in the oral tradition. Over the years poets from Wordsworth to Longfellow had appropriated the form, either as a narrative device or as a means of suggesting simplicity. Kipling himself had written some traditional "literary" ballads, such as his romantic evocation of Pathan nobility in the "Ballad of East and West."

Now he turned the form to describing the experiences of his soldier friends and heroes—from their proud familiarity with their guns ("Screw-Guns"), through the cussedness of camels in the baggage trains ("Oonts"), to the pleasures of service life abroad ("Mandalay").

From February to July 1890, thirteen Barrack-Room Ballads were published in *Scots Observer*. In chronological order these were: "Danny Deever," "Tommy," "Fuzzy-Wuzzy," "Oonts," "Loot," "Soldier, Soldier," "The Sons of the Widow" (which Kipling later renamed "The Widow at Windsor"), "Troopin'," "Gunga Din," "Mandalay," "The Young British Soldier," "Screw-Guns" and "Belts."

Because Kipling's best friend in London was the American publisher Wolcott Balestier, these ballads were first published in book form not in London but in New York, where the United States Book Company brought out an edition of *Departmental Ditties, Barrack-Room Ballads and Other Verses* in December 1890—an introductory omnibus for the American market, incorporating some of the witty poems Kipling had written in India, as well as his more recent ballads.

Over the next year or so Kipling continued to write Barrack-Room Ballads, but not in the intense manner of those early months of 1890. He was also writing stories, different types of verse, and even a couple of novels (one, *The Naulahka,* with Balestier). However, in December 1891, Balestier died of typhoid fever in Germany, causing Kipling great grief. To the astonishment of mutual friends, including Henry James, Kipling abruptly married Balestier's sister Carrie and moved across the Atlantic to her home town of Brattleboro in Vermont.

By then he had composed a further seven soldiers' songs, which appeared with the original thirteen and many others in *Barrack-Room Ballads and Other Verses,* published by Methuen in London and Macmillan in New York in March 1892 (the month after his marriage to Carrie). This edition also contained an emotional dedication to Wolcott Balestier.

While writing other works, such as *The Jungle Books,* in his self-built house in Brattleboro, Kipling continued to produce occasional Barrack-Room Ballads. He sent them to magazines, such as the *Pall Mall Gazette* in London, and later included them all (by now an additional seventeen) in a special section at the end of his next book of poems, *The Seven Seas,* published by D. Appleton and Company in a limited copyright edition in New York in September 1896 and by Methuen in London two months later.

This later group of seventeen poems does not have the force of his original Barrack-Room Ballads. To an extent, they reflect the nostalgia of an Englishman living in Vermont for the imperial, military life. One or two have nothing to do with the army at all—"Bill 'Awkins" is more of a music hall ditty, while "The Mother-Lodge" comes in the category of "fond recollection." However they do include certain poems that can rank with his earlier soldiers' songs. "The Ladies" is a sophisticated take on the joys of eclectic sexual experience, "The Sergeant's Weddin' " offers a typically cheeky insight into the behavior of noncommissioned officers, "The Shut-Eye Sentry" is another amusing behind-the-scenes look at regimental life, while "Mary, Pity Women!" brings together the music hall, emotional longing and religion.

Looked at in their entirety, the thirty-seven Barrack-Room Ballads provide a journalistic overview of British army life in the late nineteenth century. Sometimes specific poems, such as "The Men That Fought at Minden" or "Snarleyow," look back to earlier campaigns, but that is in the nature of ballads—a poetic form that tends to emphasize the continuity of experience, with the same themes continually arising in these tales of barrack-room existence, action in the field and the pain of being away from one's loved ones.

Kipling ranges over different categories of military service, writing about the engineers ("Sapper"), gunners ("Screw-Guns") and marines ("Soldier an' Sailor Too"). He has something to say about most stages of a soldier's life from recruitment ("The Young British Soldier") through instruction ("The Men That Fought at Minden") to going home ("Troopin' ") and later reflecting on their military experience ("Mandalay"), and even trying to sign up again ("Back to the Army Again"). He is good on local color, as in "Gentleman-Rankers," but does not gloss over horrors ("Cholera Camp") or even politically incorrect practices ("Loot"). While focusing on the camaraderie of soldiers ("Gunga Din"), their antics in the barracks ("The Shut-Eye Sentry"), their drunkenness ("Cells"), their brawling ("Belts") and their experience in battle ("Snarleyow"), he does not ignore the woman's role in a soldier's life—usually as the person left behind ("Mary, Pity Women!"), sometimes a snatched but generally much valued love on the road ("The Ladies").

While the effect is sympathetic to the army's

involvement in British imperialism, Kipling is not afraid to point out the negative reactions of the rank and file: sometimes they fail to understand what they are fighting for ("The Widow's Party") or they resent the condescension and hypocrisy of civilians who seem to love them when they are going off to fight but otherwise scorn or ignore them ("Tommy").

For the "background accompaniment" to his poetry, Kipling drew on all types of music familiar to the army man, from hymns ("The 'Eathen") through the bugle in "The Widow's Party" and the drum beats in "Danny Deever" or "Route Marchin' " to the ritual funeral march of "Follow Me 'Ome."

For the poetic heart of his output, Kipling looked to popular ballads (Scottish border ballads, in particular), though he gave them his own contemporary gloss. On one level, he did this through his use of colloquialisms and dialect, incorporating Cockney, Irish, military and a sprinkling of Hindustani phrases. This was often shocking to critics brought up in the literary tradition of Tennyson (whose "Charge of the Light Brigade" was an earlier foray into army subject matter). On the other, he was skillful in his adaptation of ballad meters—a point recognized by T. S. Eliot, who wrote enthusiastically about the "combination of heavy beat and variation of pace" in "Danny Deever," "a poem which is technically (as well as in content) remarkable. The regular recurrence of the same end-words, which gain immensely by imperfect rhyme (*parade* and *said*) gives the feeling of marching feet and the movement of men in disciplined formation—in a unity of movement which enhances the horror of the occasion and the sickness which seizes the men as individuals; and the slightly quickened pace of the final lines marks the changes in movement and in music." (*A Choice of Kipling's Verse*)

Eliot noted the appositeness of the word "whimpers" at that poem's end:

"What's that that whimpers over'ead?" said Files-
on-Parade.
"It's Danny's soul that's passin' now," the
Colour-Sergeant said.

Eliot may well have recalled this in his famous line
in "The Hollow Men":

This is the way the world ends
Not with a bang but with a whimper.

If nothing else, Eliot's comments show that Kip-
ling's achievement in *Barrack-Room Ballads* was re-
spected by his peers. Kipling's poetic snapshots of war
were very different from the more lugubrious reflec-
tions that were to be sent home by participants in
the First World War. Although his soldiers had their
complaints, they tended to look back with some satis-
faction on their military careers, even if the bottom
line was the imperialist project conveyed in "The Wid-
ow's Party":

We broke a King and we built a road—
A court-house stands where the reg'ment goed.
And the river's clean where the raw blood
flowed. . . .

—Andrew Lycett

BARRACK-ROOM
BALLADS

To T. A.°

With their familiar, faintly amused tone, Kipling's intro-
ductory stanzas underline his admiration for the British
fighting soldier.

    I have made for you a song,
    And it may be right or wrong,
But only you can tell me if it's true;
    I have tried for to explain
    Both your pleasure and your pain,   5
And, Thomas, here's my best respects to you!

    O there'll surely come a day
    When they'll give you all your pay,
And treat you as a Christian ought to do;
    So, until that day comes round,   10
    Heaven keep you safe and sound,
And, Thomas, here's my best respects to you!

                    R. K.

—*First published in* Barrack-Room Ballads and
              Other Verses *(London, 1892)*

T. A. Tommy (or Thomas) Atkins had developed during the
nineteenth century into a generic name for the ordinary British
soldier; its origin remains uncertain. According to one version,
the Duke of Wellington, the victor at the Battle of Waterloo
(1815), coined the usage, recalling a mortally injured grenadier
of that name. However, in *The Search for Thomas Atkins*
(1945), Robert Graves suggested that the name first appeared
in a War Office order of 31 August 1815 that referred to
Thomas Atkins of Odiham in Hampshire, a member of No. 6
Company, 1st Battalion, 23rd Regiment of Foot.

Danny Deever

Kipling's first poem published specifically as a Barrack-Room Ballad. This traditional English question-and-answer ballad poem evokes the unremitting nature of the heat, discipline and underlying terror experienced by the British soldier in India. By the time it was written, however, public executions had been banned. The last one in civilian life took place in 1866.

"What are the bugles blowin' for?" said Files-
    on-Parade.°
"To turn you out, to turn you out," the Colour-
    Sergeant said.
"What makes you look so white, so white?" said
    Files-on-Parade.
"I'm dreadin' what I've got to watch," the Colour-
    Sergeant said.
        For they're hangin' Danny Deever, you
           can hear the Dead March play,   5
        The regiment's in 'ollow square—they're
           hangin' him to-day;
        They've taken of his buttons off an' cut
           his stripes away,
        An' they're hangin' Danny Deever in
           the mornin'.

"What makes the rear-rank breathe so 'ard?" said
    Files-on-Parade.
"It's bitter cold, it's bitter cold," the Colour-
    Sergeant said.   10
"What makes that front-rank man fall down?"
    said Files-on-Parade.

1 **Files-on-Parade** British troops generally paraded in two files, which could be arranged in various formations including " 'ollow square," that is, a squared-off U shape, facing inward.

4

"A touch o' sun, a touch o' sun," the Colour-
    Sergeant said.
       They are hangin' Danny Deever, they are
marchin' of 'im round,
       They 'ave 'alted Danny Deever by 'is
coffin on the ground;
       An' 'e'll swing in 'arf a minute for a
sneakin' shootin' hound—   15
       O they're hangin' Danny Deever in the
mornin'!

" 'Is cot was right-'and cot to mine," said Files-
    on-Parade.
" 'E's sleepin' out an' far to-night," the Colour-
    Sergeant said.
"I've drunk 'is beer a score o' times," said Files-
    on-Parade.
" 'E's drinkin' bitter beer alone," the Colour-
    Sergeant said.   20
       They are hangin' Danny Deever, you must
         mark 'im to 'is place,
       For 'e shot a comrade sleepin'—you must
         look 'im in the face;
       Nine 'undred of 'is county an' the
         regiment's disgrace,
       While they're hangin' Danny Deever in
         the mornin'.

"What's that so black agin' the sun?" said Files-
    on-Parade.   25
"It's Danny fightin' 'ard for life," the Colour-
    Sergeant said.
"What's that that whimpers over'ead?" said Files-
    on-Parade.
"It's Danny's soul that's passin' now," the Colour-
    Sergeant said.
       For they're done with Danny Deever, you
         can 'ear the quickstep play,

The regiment's in column, an' they're
    marchin' us away;   *30*
Ho! the young recruits are shakin', an'
    they'll want their beer to-day,
After hangin' Danny Deever in the mornin'.

—*First published in* The Scots Observer
                (22 February 1890)

Tommy

Adopting a typical Kipling pose—part cynical, part amused resignation—the speaker of the poem describes how the enlisted soldier (Thomas Atkins or T. A.—see p. 3) is feted when he is needed to fight, but is otherwise poorly treated by the general public.

I went into a public-'ouse to get a pint o' beer,
The publican 'e up an' sez, "We serve no red-
    coats here."
The girls be'ind the bar they laughed an' giggled
    fit to die,
I outs into the street again an' to myself sez I:
      O it's Tommy this, an' Tommy that, an'
          "Tommy, go away";   5
      But it's "Thank you, Mister Atkins," when
          the band begins to play,
      The band begins to play, my boys, the band
          begins to play,
      O it's "Thank you, Mister Atkins," when the
          band begins to play.

I went into a theatre as sober as could be,
They gave a drunk civilian room, but 'adn't none
    for me;   10
They sent me to the gallery or round the music-
    'alls,
But when it comes to fightin', Lord! they'll shove
    me in the stalls!
      For it's Tommy this, an' Tommy that, an'
          "Tommy, wait outside";
      But it's "Special train for Atkins" when the
          trooper's on the tide,
      The troopship's on the tide, my boys, the
          troopship's on the tide,   15
      O it's "Special train for Atkins" when the
          trooper's on the tide.

Yes, makin' mock o' uniforms that guard you
    while you sleep
Is cheaper than them uniforms, an' they're
    starvation cheap;
An' hustlin' drunken soldiers when they're goin'
    large a bit
Is five times better business than paradin' in full
    kit.   20
    Then it's Tommy this, an' Tommy that, an'
        "Tommy, 'ow's yer soul?"
    But it's "Thin red line of 'eroes"° when the
        drums begin to roll,
    The drums begin to roll, my boys, the drums
        begin to roll,
    O it's "Thin red line of 'eroes" when the
        drums begin to roll.

We aren't no thin red 'eroes, nor we aren't no
    blackguards too,   25
But single men in barricks, most remarkable like
    you;
An' if sometimes our conduck isn't all your
    fancy paints,
Why, single men in barricks don't grow into
    plaster saints;
    While it's Tommy this, an' Tommy that, an'
        "Tommy, fall be'ind,"
    But it's "Please to walk in front, sir," when
        there's trouble in the wind,   30
    There's trouble in the wind, my boys, there's
        trouble in the wind,
    O it's "Please to walk in front, sir," when
        there's trouble in the wind.

22 **"Thin red line of 'eroes"** W. H. Russell, correspondent for
The Times of London, coined this phrase during the Crimean
War to describe the scarlet-clad double line of the 93rd
Highlanders standing firm against the Russian cavalry at the
battle of Balaclava on 25 October 1854.

You talk o' better food for us, an' schools, an'
      fires, an' all:
We'll wait for extry rations if you treat us rational.
Don't mess about the cook-room slops, but prove
      it to our face   *35*
The Widow's Uniform is not the soldier-man's
      disgrace.
    For it's Tommy this, an' Tommy that, an'
      "Chuck him out, the brute!"
    But it's "Saviour of 'is country" when the guns
      begin to shoot;
    An' it's Tommy this, an' Tommy that, an'
      anything you please;
    An' Tommy ain't a bloomin' fool—you bet
      that Tommy sees!   *40*

          —First published in The Scots Observer
                         (1 March 1890)

"Fuzzy-Wuzzy"°

Although the popular perception of Kipling's poetry may be that it is condescending to the non-British, these verses reflect the British soldier's respect for the abilities of his opponents.

We've fought with many men acrost the seas,
    An' some of 'em was brave an' some was not:
The Paythan an' the Zulu an' Burmese;
    But the Fuzzy was the finest o' the lot.
We never got a ha'porth's change of 'im: 5
    'E squatted in the scrub an' 'ocked our 'orses,
'E cut our sentries up at Sua*kim*,
    An' 'e played the cat an' banjo with our forces.
        So 'ere's *to* you, Fuzzy-Wuzzy, at your
            'ome in the Soudan;
        You're a pore benighted 'eathen but a
            first-class fightin' man;   10
        We gives you your certificate, an' if you
            want it signed
        We'll come an' 'ave a romp with you
            whenever you're inclined.

We took our chanst among the Khyber 'ills,
    The Boers knocked us silly at a mile,
The Burman give us Irriwaddy chills,   15
    An' a Zulu *impi* dished us up in style:
But all we ever got from such as they
    Was pop to what the Fuzzy made us swaller;
We 'eld our bloomin' own, the papers say,
    But man for man the Fuzzy knocked us 'oller.   20
        Then 'ere's *to* you, Fuzzy-Wuzzy, an' the
            missis an' the kid;
        Our orders was to break you, an' of
            course we went an' did.

Fuzzy-Wuzzy military nickname for the Hadendowa, a tribe in Eastern Sudan who wore their hair in a frizzed-out style that today might be termed an "Afro"

We sloshed you with Martinis, an' it
    wasn't 'ardly fair;
But for all the odds agin' you, Fuzzy-
    Wuz, you broke the square.°

'E 'asn't got no papers of 'is own,   *25*
    'E 'asn't got no medals nor rewards,
So we must certify the skill 'e's shown
    In usin' of 'is long two-'anded swords:
When 'e's 'oppin' in an' out among the bush
    With 'is coffin-'eaded shield an' shovel-spear,   *30*
An 'appy day with Fuzzy on the rush
    Will last an 'ealthy Tommy for a year.
        So 'ere's *to* you, Fuzzy-Wuzzy, an' your
            friends which are no more,
        If we 'adn't lost some messmates we
            would 'elp you to deplore;
        But give an' take's the gospel, an' we'll
            call the bargain fair,   *35*
        For if you 'ave lost more than us, you
            crumpled up the square!

'E rushes at the smoke when we let drive,
    An', before we know, 'e's 'ackin' at our 'ead;
'E's all 'ot sand an' ginger when alive,
    An' 'e's generally shammin' when 'e's dead.   *40*
'E's a daisy, 'e's a ducky, 'e's a lamb!
    'E's a injia-rubber idiot on the spree,
'E's the on'y thing that doesn't give a damn
    For a Regiment o' British Infantree!
        So 'ere's *to* you, Fuzzy-Wuzzy, at your
            'ome in the Soudan;   *45*
        You're a pore benighted 'eathen but a
            first-class fightin' man;

24 broke the square On 24 December 1884, during Britain's war
against the Sudanese military-religious leader, the Mahdi, his
troops broke into British defensive lines (formed as a square) at
the Battle of Abu Klea. The Sudanese tribe involved was in fact
the Baggara. (The campaign is also described in Kipling's novel *The
Light That Failed* [1890].)

An' 'ere's *to* you, Fuzzy-Wuzzy, with
your 'ayrick 'ead of 'air—
You big black boundin' beggar—for
you broke a British square!

—*First published in* The Scots Observer
(15 March 1890)

Soldier, Soldier

A traditional ballad on the theme of women awaiting news of their men fighting abroad. A trifle sentimental, it nevertheless captures the heartbreak and regular losses experienced by those left behind.

"Soldier, soldier come from the wars,
Why don't you march with my true love?"
"We're fresh from off the ship an' 'e's maybe give
    the slip,
An' you'd best go look for a new love."

     New love! True love!   5
     Best go look for a new love,
     The dead they cannot rise, an' you'd
        better dry your eyes,
     An' you'd best go look for a new love.

"Soldier, soldier come from the wars,
What did you see o' my true love?"   10
"I seed 'im serve the Queen in a suit o' rifle-
    green,°
An' you'd best go look for a new love."

"Soldier, soldier come from the wars,
Did ye see no more o' my true love?"
"I seed 'im runnin' by when the shots begun to
    fly—   15
But you'd best go look for a new love."

"Soldier, soldier come from the wars,
Did aught take 'arm to my true love?"
"I couldn't see the fight, for the smoke it lay so
    white—
An' you'd best go look for a new love."   20

11 **a suit o' rifle-green** the uniform worn by men originally recruited to rifle regiments (including the Rifle Brigade) during the American wars of the eighteenth century

"Soldier, soldier come from the wars,
I'll up an' tend to my true love!"
" 'E's lying on the dead with a bullet through 'is
    'ead,
An' you'd best go look for a new love."

"Soldier, soldier come from the wars,   25
I'll down an' die with my true love!"
"The pit we dug'll 'ide 'im an' the twenty men
        beside 'im—
An' you'd best go look for a new love."

"Soldier, soldier come from the wars,
Do you bring no sign from my true love?"   30
"I bring a lock of 'air that 'e allus used to wear,
An' you'd best go look for a new love."

"Soldier, soldier come from the wars,
O then I know it's true I've lost my true love!"
"An' I tell you truth again—when you've lost the
        feel o' pain
You'd best take me for your true love."   35

        True love! New love!
        Best take 'im for a new love,
        The dead they cannot rise, an' you'd better
            dry your eyes,
        An' you'd best take 'im for your true love.   40

        —First published in The Scots Observer
                        (12 April 1890)

Screw-Guns

Screw-guns were the seven-pounder guns used in mountain warfare in the late nineteenth century, which could be quickly taken apart, or "unscrewed," into three pieces, plus two wheels. The poem deftly sketches the rugged terrain of the Northwest frontier.

Smokin' my pipe on the mountings, sniffin' the
    mornin' cool,
I walks in my old brown gaiters along o' my old
    brown mule,
With seventy gunners be'ind me, an' never a
    beggar forgets
It's only the pick of the Army that handles the
    dear little pets—'Tss! 'Tss!
      For you all love the screw-guns—the
        screw-guns they all love you!   5
      So when we call round with a few guns,
        o' course you will know what to do—
        hoo! hoo!
      Jest send in your Chief an' surrender—
        it's worse if you fights or you runs:
      You can go where you please, you can
        skid up the trees, but you don't get
        away from the guns!

They sends us along where the roads are, but
      mostly we goes where they ain't:
We'd climb up the side of a sign-board an' trust
      to the stick o' the paint: 10
We've chivied° the Naga an' Looshai,° we've give
      the Afreedeeman° fits,
For we fancies ourselves at two thousand, we guns
      that are built in two bits—'Tss! 'Tss!
      For you all love the screw-guns . . .

---

11 **chivied** harassed **Naga an' Looshai** hill tribes on India's Northwest frontier **Afreedeeman** the Afridi tribe

If a man doesn't work, why, we drills 'im an'
    teaches 'im 'ow to behave;
If a beggar can't march, why, we kills 'im an'
    rattles 'im into 'is grave.   15
You've got to stand up to our business an' spring
    without snatchin' or fuss.
D'you say that you sweat with the field-guns?
    By God, you must lather with us—'Tss! 'Tss!
        For you all love the screw-guns . . .

The eagles is screamin' around us, the river's a-
    moanin' below,
We're clear o' the pine an' the oak-scrub,
    we're out on the rocks an' the snow,   20
An' the wind is as thin as a whip-lash what carries
    away to the plains
The rattle an' stamp o' the lead-mules—the
    jinglety-jink o' the chains—'Tss! 'Tss!
        For you all love the screw-guns . . .

There's a wheel on the Horns o' the Mornin', an'
    a wheel on the edge o' the Pit,°
An' a drop into nothin' beneath you as straight
    as a beggar can spit: 25
With the sweat runnin' out o' your shirt-sleeves,
    an' the sun off the snow in your face,
An' 'arf o' the men on the drag-ropes to hold the
    old gun in 'er place—'Tss! 'Tss!
        For you all love the screw-guns . . .

24 **Horns o' the Mornin' . . . the Pit** The horns of the morning
are the peaks of the hills on one side of the precipitous
mountain path; the pit is the ravine on the other. In a letter
of 6 March 1890, quoted in Professor Thomas Pinney's edition
of Kipling's Letters (vol 2, p.10), Kipling refers to having
"walked 'with Death and morning on the silver horns' in the
Himalayas." Professor Pinney notes that Kipling's own
quotation came from Tennyson's The Princess, VII, l. 189. The
pit has the added meaning of death, oblivion and even hell.
*(With thanks to Lisa Lewis, Colonel Roger Ayers and others at
www.kipling.org.uk)*

Smokin' my pipe on the mountings, sniffin' the
    mornin' cool,
I climbs in my old brown gaiters along o' my old
    brown mule.   30
The monkey can say what our road was—
    the wild-goat 'e knows where we passed.
Stand easy, you long-eared old darlin's! Out
    drag-ropes!
    With shrapnel! Hold fast—'Tss! 'Tss!
        For you all love the screw-guns—the
            screw-guns they all love you!
        So when we take tea with a few guns, o'
            course you will know what to do—
            hoo! hoo!   35
        Jest send in your Chief an' surrender—it's
            worse if you fights or you runs:
        You may hide in the caves, they'll be only
            your graves, but you can't get away
            from the guns!

           —*First published in* The Scots Observer
                       (12 July 1890)

Cells

This ballad captures the remorse of the soldier who has been reprimanded for being "drunk and resisting the Guard." He has a fearful hangover, has lost most parts of his uniform and must face his wife and child at the gate of the barracks.

I've a head like a concertina: I've a tongue like a
    button-stick:
I've a mouth like an old potato, and I'm more
    than a little sick,
But I've had my fun o' the Corp'ral's Guard: I've
    made the cinders fly,
And I'm here in the Clink° for a thundering drink
    and blacking the Corporal's eye.

        With a second-hand overcoat under
            my head,
          And a beautiful view of the yard,   5
     O it's pack-drill for me and a fortnight's
            C.B.°
        For "drunk and resisting the Guard!"
        Mad drunk and resisting the Guard—
        'Strewth, but I socked it them hard!   10
     So it's pack-drill for me and a fortnight's
            C.B.
        For "drunk and resisting the Guard."

I started o' canteen porter, I finished o' canteen
    beer,
But a dose o' gin that a mate slipped in, it was
    that that brought me here.
'Twas that and an extry double Guard that rubbed
    my nose in the dirt;   15
But I fell away with the Corp'ral's stock and the
    best of the Corp'ral's shirt.

4 **Clink** military prison   7 **C.B.** confined to barracks

Cells

I left my cap in a public-house, my boots in the
 public road,
And Lord knows where, and I don't care, my belt
 and my tunic goed;
They'll stop my pay, they'll cut away the stripes I
 used to wear,
But I left my mark on the Corp'ral's face, and I
 think he'll keep it there!   20

My wife she cries on the barrack-gate, my kid in
 the barrack-yard,
It ain't that I mind the Ord'ly room—it's *that* that
 cuts so hard.
I'll take my oath before them both that I will
 sure abstain,
But as soon as I'm in with a mate and gin, I know
 I'll do it again!

     With a second-hand overcoat under
        my head,   25
        And a beautiful view of the yard,
   Yes, it's pack-drill for me and a
        fortnight's C.B.
        For "drunk and resisting the Guard!"
        Mad drunk and resisting the Guard—
        'Strewth, but I socked it them hard!   30
   So it's pack-drill for me and a fortnight's
        C.B.
        For "drunk and resisting the Guard."

—*First published in* The National Observer
(29 November 1890)

Gunga Din

On this occasion Kipling praises the bravery and altruism of a humble native water carrier—supposedly based on Juma, a particularly courageous water carrier attached to the Corps of Guides during the siege of Delhi in the Indian mutiny of July 1857.

You may talk o' gin and beer
When you're quartered safe out 'ere,
An' you're sent to penny-fights an' Aldershot it;°
But when it comes to slaughter
You will do your work on water,   5
An' you'll lick the bloomin' boots of 'im that's
    got it.
Now in Injia's sunny clime,
Where I used to spend my time
A-servin' of 'Er Majesty the Queen,
Of all them blackfaced crew   10
The finest man I knew
Was our regimental bhisti,° Gunga Din.
      He was "Din! Din! Din!
   You limpin' lump o' brick-dust, Gunga Din!
      Hi! slippery *hitherao*!   15
        Water, get it! *Panee lao!*°
  You squidgy-nosed old idol, Gunga Din."

The uniform 'e wore
Was nothin' much before,
An' rather less than 'arf o' that be'ind,   20
For a piece o' twisty rag
An' a goatskin water-bag
Was all the field-equipment 'e could find.
When the sweatin' troop-train lay
In a sidin' through the day,   25

3 **Aldershot it** take it easy (that is, be in Aldershot, a leading garrison town in Surrey, as opposed to being in India)   12 **bhisti** water carrier (Hindustani)   16 *Panee lao* bring water swiftly

Where the 'eat would make your bloomin'
    eyebrows crawl,
We shouted "Harry By!"°
Till our throats were bricky-dry,
Then we wopped 'im 'cause 'e couldn't serve us all.
        It was "Din! Din! Din!   30
   You 'eathen, where the mischief 'ave you been?
      You put some *juldee*° in it
      Or I'll *marrow*° you this minute
  If you don't fill up my helmet, Gunga Din!"

'E would dot an' carry one   35
Till the longest day was done;
An' 'e didn't seem to know the use o' fear.
If we charged or broke or cut,
You could bet your bloomin' nut,
'E'd be waitin' fifty paces right flank rear.   40
With 'is *mussick*° on 'is back,
'E would skip with our attack,
An' watch us till the bugles made "Retire,"
An' for all 'is dirty 'ide
'E was white, clear white, inside   45
When 'e went to tend the wounded under fire!
        It was "Din! Din! Din!"
  With the bullets kickin' dust-spots on the green.
      When the cartridges ran out,
      You could hear the front-files shout,   50
  "Hi! ammunition-mules an' Gunga Din!"

I shan't forgit the night
When I dropped be'ind the fight
With a bullet where my belt-plate should 'a' been.
I was chokin' mad with thirst,   55
An' the man that spied me first
Was our good old grinnin', gruntin' Gunga Din.

27 **Harry By** British army slang equivalent to "oh, brother"
32 *juldee* speed   33 *marrow* hit   41 *mussick* (musick) goatskin
water bag (made from goat because pigskin would offend
Muslims and cow's leather Hindus)

'E lifted up my 'ead,
An' 'e plugged me where I bled,
An' 'e guv me 'arf-a-pint o' water-green: 60
It was crawlin' and it stunk,
But of all the drinks I've drunk,
I'm gratefullest to one from Gunga Din.
            It was "Din! Din! Din!
    'Ere's a beggar with a bullet through 'is spleen; 65
            'E's chawin' up the ground,
            An' 'e's kickin' all around:
    For Gawd's sake git the water, Gunga Din!"

'E carried me away
To where a dooli° lay,   70
An' a bullet come an' drilled the beggar clean.
'E put me safe inside,
An' just before 'e died,
"I 'ope you liked your drink," sez Gunga Din.
So I'll meet 'im later on   75
At the place where 'e is gone—
Where it's always double drill and no canteen;
'E'll be squattin' on the coals
Givin' drink to poor damned souls,
An' I'll get a swig in hell from Gunga Din!   80
            Yes, Din! Din! Din!
    You Lazarushian-leather Gunga Din!
            Though I've belted you and flayed you,
            By the livin' Gawd that made you,
    You're a better man than I am, Gunga Din!   85

            —*First published in* The Scots Observer
                        (7 June 1890)

70 **dooli** stretcher

Oonts

(Northern India Transport Train)

*"Unt" is the Hindustani word for camel, usually
pronounced with the sound of the "u" in "bull" but
by the Cockney speaker of the poem like the "u" in
"bunt." The poem reflects the annoyance felt by the
soldier in charge of the baggage train at the behavior
of the Indian army's main beast of burden.*

Wot makes the soldier's 'eart to penk,° wot makes
      'im to perspire?
It isn't standin' up to charge nor lyin' down to fire;
But it's everlastin' waitin' on a everlastin' road
For the commissariat° camel an' 'is commissariat
      load.
      O the oont, O the oont, O the
          commissariat oont!   5
        With 'is silly neck a-bobbin' like a
          basket full o' snakes;
        We packs 'im like an idol, an' you ought
          to 'ear 'im grunt,
        An' when we gets 'im loaded up 'is
          blessed girth-rope breaks.

Wot makes the rear-guard swear so 'ard when
      night is drorin' in,
An' every native follower is shiverin' for 'is skin?   *10*
It ain't the chanst o' being rushed by Paythans°
      from the 'ills,
It's the commissariat camel puttin' on 'is
      bloomin' frills!
        O the oont, O the oont, O the hairy
          scary oont!

1 **penk** palpitate (analogous to the engine of a car "pinking," or
stuttering, through the wrong mixture of fuel) 4 **commissariat**
the section of the army responsible for serving and in this case
transporting food and essential supplies 11 **Paythans** the
Pathan tribe

A-trippin' over tent-ropes when we've
    got the night alarm!
We socks 'im with a stretcher-pole an' 'eads
    'im off in front,   15
    An' when we've saved 'is bloomin' life 'e
        chaws our bloomin' arm.

The 'orse 'e knows above a bit, the bullock's but
    a fool,
The elephant's a gentleman, the battery-mule's a
    mule;
But the commissariat cam-u-el, when all is said
    an' done,
'E's a devil an' a ostrich an' a orphan-child in one.   20
        O the oont, O the oont, O the Gawd-
            forsaken oont!
          The lumpy-'umpy 'ummin'-bird a-singin'
            where 'e lies,
        'E's blocked the whole division from the
          rear-guard to the front,
          An' when we get 'im up again—the
            beggar goes an' dies!

'E'll gall an' chafe° an' lame an' fight—'e smells
    most awful vile;   25
'E'll lose 'isself for ever if you let 'im stray a mile;
'E's game to graze the 'ole day long an' 'owl the
    'ole night through,
An' when 'e comes to greasy ground 'e splits
    'isself in two.
        O the oont, O the oont, O the floppin',
            droppin' oont!
          When 'is long legs give from under an'
            'is meltin' eye is dim,   30
        The tribes is up be'ind us, and the tribes is
          out in front—
          It ain't no jam for Tommy, but it's kites
            an' crows for 'im.

25 **gall an' chafe** get sore (around the saddle) through rubbing

So when the cruel march is done, an' when the
    roads is blind,
An' when we sees the camp in front an' 'ears the
    shots be'ind,
Ho! then we strips 'is saddle off, and all 'is woes
    is past: 35
'E thinks on us that used 'im so, and gets revenge
    at last.
    O the oont, O the oont, O the floatin',
        bloatin' oont!
      The late lamented camel in the water-cut
        'e lies;
    We keeps a mile be'ind 'im an' we keeps a
        mile in front,
      But 'e gets into the drinkin'-casks, and
        then o' course we dies.   40

    —*First published in* The Scots Observer
               (22 March 1890)

Loot

This poem is often considered one of the more outrageous in Kipling's oeuvre, because of the enthusiasm it conveys for the business of looting. However, it is a good example of Kipling the journalist reporting a feature of the contemporary fighting experience without necessarily subscribing to it.

If you've ever stole a pheasant-egg be'ind the
      keeper's back,
    If you've ever snigged the washin' from the
      line,
If you've ever crammed a gander in your
      bloomin' 'aversack,
    You will understand this little song o' mine.
But the service rules are 'ard, an' from such we
    are debarred,   5
    For the same with English morals does not
      suit.
            (*Cornet*: Toot! toot!)—
W'y, they call a man a robber if 'e stuffs 'is
    marchin' clobber°
    With the—
(*Chorus*) Loo! loo! Lulu! lulu! Loo! loo! Loot!°
    loot! loot!   10
             Ow the loot!
             Bloomin' loot!
    That's the thing to make the boys git up
      an' shoot!
      It's the same with dogs an' men,
      If you'd make 'em come again   15
    Clap 'em forward with a Loo! loo!
      Lulu! Loot!
  (*ff*)°   Whoopee! Tear 'im, puppy! Loo! loo!
      Lulu! Loot! loot! loot!

---

8 **clobber** clothes 10 **Loot** The common English word "loot" derives from "lut," Hindustani for plunder. 18 *ff* fortissimo or very loud

If you've knocked a nigger edgeways when 'e's
    thrustin' for your life,
  You must leave 'im very careful where 'e fell;
An' may thank your stars an' gaiters if you didn't
    feel 'is knife   20
  That you ain't told off to bury 'im as well.
Then the sweatin' Tommies wonder as they spade
    the beggars under
  Why lootin' should be entered as a crime;
So if my song you'll 'ear, I will learn you plain
    an' clear
  'Ow to pay yourself for fightin' overtime.   25
(*Chorus*) With the loot, . . .

Now remember when you're 'acking round a
    gilded Burma god
  That 'is eyes is very often precious stones;
An' if you treat a nigger to a dose o' cleanin'-rod
  'E's like to show you everything 'e owns.   30
When 'e won't prodooce no more, pour some
    water on the floor
  Where you 'ear it answer 'ollow to the boot
    (*Cornet*: Toot! toot!)—
When the ground begins to sink, shove your
    baynick° down the chink,
  An' you're sure to touch the—   35
(*Chorus*) Loo! loo! Lulu! Loot! loot! loot!
    Ow the loot! . . .

When from 'ouse to 'ouse you're 'unting, you
    must always work in pairs—
  It 'alves the gain, but safer you will find—
For a single man gets bottled on them twisty-
    wisty stairs,   40
  An' a woman comes and clobs 'im from be'ind.
When you've turned 'em inside out, an' it seems
    beyond a doubt

34 baynick bayonet

As if there weren't enough to dust a flute
      (*Cornet*: Toot! toot!)—
Before you sling your 'ook,° at the 'ousetops take
    a look,   45
For it's underneath the tiles they 'ide the loot.
(*Chorus*) Ow the loot! . . .

You can mostly square a Sergint an' a
      Quartermaster too,
If you only take the proper way to go;
I could never keep my pickin's, but I've learned
    you all I knew—   50
An' don't you never say I told you so.
An' now I'll bid good-bye, for I'm gettin' rather
    dry,
An' I see another tunin' up to toot
      (*Cornet*: Toot! toot!)—
So 'ere's good-luck to those that wears the
    Widow's clo'es,   55
An' the Devil send 'em all they want o' loot!
(*Chorus*)   Yes, the loot,
        Bloomin' loot!
   In the tunic an' the mess-tin an' the boot!
   It's the same with dogs an' men,   60
   If you'd make 'em come again
(*fff*)°   Whoop 'em forward with a Loo! loo!
    Lulu! Loot! loot! loot!
Heeya! Sick 'im, puppy! Loo! loo! Lulu!
    Loot! loot! loot!

    —*First published in* The Scots Observer
        (29 March 1890)

---

45 **sling your 'ook** move off, decamp, probably because
soldiers used to carry their baggage on a hook on the end of
a stick   62 *fff* fortississimo or as loud as possible

"Snarleyow"°

The incident in this ballad took place during the First Sikh War at the battle of Ferozeshah on 21 December 1845. It is described in Sergeant N. W. Bancroft's memoir From Recruit to Staff Sergeant, *a book published in 1885 and reviewed by Kipling while he was in India.*

This 'appened in a battle to a batt'ry of the corps
Which is first among the women an' amazin' first
    in war;
An' what the bloomin' battle was I don't
    remember now,
But Two's off-lead° 'e answered to the name o'
    Snarleyow.
      Down in the Infantry, nobody cares;   5
      Down in the Cavalry, Colonel 'e swears;
      But down in the lead with the wheel at
        the flog
      Turns the bold Bombardier to a little
        whipped dog!

They was movin' into action, they was needed
    very sore,
To learn a little schoolin' to a native army corps,   10
They 'ad nipped against an uphill, they was tuckin'
    down the brow,
When a tricky, trundlin' roundshot give the knock
    to *Snarleyow.*

They cut 'im loose an' left 'im—'e was almost tore
    in two—
But he tried to follow after as a well-trained 'orse
    should do;
'E went an' fouled the limber, an' the Driver's
    Brother squeals: 15

"Snarleyow" The name derives from the novel *Snarleyow,* written in 1837 by Captain Frederick Marryat. **4 Two's off-lead** the lead offside horse pulling Number Two gun

"Pull up, pull up for *Snarleyow*—'is head's
    between 'is 'eels!"

The Driver 'umped 'is shoulder, for the wheels
    was goin' round,
An' there ain't no "Stop, conductor!" when a
    batt'ry's changin' ground;
Sez 'e: "I broke the beggar in, an' very sad I feels,
But I couldn't pull up, not for *you*—your 'ead
    between your 'eels!"   20

'E 'adn't 'ardly spoke the word, before a
    droppin' shell
A little right the batt'ry an' between the sections
    fell;
An' when the smoke 'ad cleared away, before the
    limber wheels,
There lay the Driver's Brother with 'is 'ead
    between 'is 'eels.

Then sez the Driver's Brother, an' 'is words was
    very plain,   25
"For Gawd's own sake get over me, an' put me
    out o' pain."
They saw 'is wounds was mortial, an' they judged
    that it was best,
So they took an' drove the limber straight across
    'is back an' chest.

The Driver 'e give nothin' 'cept a little coughin'
    grunt,
But 'e swung 'is 'orses 'andsome when it came to
    "Action Front!"   30
An' if one wheel was juicy, you may lay your
    Monday head
'Twas juicier for the niggers when the case begun
    to spread.

The moril of this story, it is plainly to be seen:
You 'avn't got no families when servin' of the
    Queen—

"Snarleyow"

You 'avn't got no brothers, fathers, sisters, wives,
    or sons—   *35*
If you want to win your battles take an' work your
    bloomin' guns!
        Down in the Infantry, nobody cares;
        Down in the Cavalry, Colonel 'e swears;
        But down in the lead with the wheel at
           the flog
        Turns the bold Bombardier to a little
           whipped dog!   *40*

—First published in The National Observer
        (29 November 1890)

The Widow at Windsor

A subtle evocation of the mixed emotions of the soldiers serving Queen Victoria (the Widow at Windsor) from their stations halfway around the world. On the one hand, they are proud to represent their country; on the other, they realize, with a touch of cynicism and bitterness, that they are pawns in a much bigger political game.

'Ave you 'eard o' the Widow at Windsor
  With a hairy gold crown on 'er 'ead?
She 'as ships on the foam—she 'as millions at
    'ome,
  An' she pays us poor beggars in red.
    (Ow, poor beggars in red!)   5
There's 'er nick on the cavalry 'orses,
  There's 'er mark on the medical stores—
An' 'er troopers you'll find with a fair wind be'ind
  That takes us to various wars.
    (Poor beggars!—barbarious wars!)   10
      Then 'ere's to the Widow at Windsor,
        An' 'ere's to the stores an' the guns,
    The men an' the 'orses what makes up
      the forces
      O' Missis Victorier's sons.
    (Poor beggars! Victorier's sons!)   15

Walk wide o' the Widow at Windsor,
  For 'alf o' Creation she owns:
We 'ave bought 'er the same with the sword an'
    the flame,
  An' we've salted it down with our bones.
    (Poor beggars!—it's blue with our bones!)   20
Hands off o' the sons o' the Widow,
  Hands off o' the goods in 'er shop,
For the Kings must come down an' the
    Emperors frown
  When the Widow at Windsor says "Stop"!

(Poor beggars!—we're sent to say "Stop"!)   25
    Then 'ere's to the Lodge o' the Widow,
      From the Pole to the Tropics it runs—
    To the Lodge that we tile with the rank
      an' the file,
      An' open in form with the guns.
    (Poor beggars!—it's always they guns!)   30

We 'ave 'eard o' the Widow at Windsor,
  It's safest to let 'er alone:
For 'er sentries we stand by the sea an' the land
  Wherever the bugles are blown.
    (Poor beggars!—an' don't we get blown!)   35
Take 'old o' the Wings o' the Mornin','°
  An' flop round the earth till you're dead;
But you won't get away from the tune that they
  play°
  The bloomin' old rag° over'ead.
    (Poor beggars!—it's 'ot over'ead!)   40
    Then 'ere's to the sons o' the Widow,
      Wherever, 'owever they roam.
    'Ere's all they desire, an' if they require
      A speedy return to their 'ome.
    (Poor beggars!—they'll never see 'ome!)   45

    —First published in The Scots Observer
    (26 April 1890) as "The Sons of the Widow"

36 Wings o' the Mornin' Psalms 139:9 ("If I take the wings of
the morning/And dwell in the utmost parts of the sea")
38 tune that they play the national anthem **39 bloomin' old
rag** the Union Jack

Belts

The last of the original thirteen Barrack-Room Ballads, "Belts" tells of a brawl between a British and an Irish regiment stationed in Dublin (the topography of which is clear from references to Silver Street, the river Liffey and Phoenix Park).

There was a row in Silver Street that's near to
    Dublin Quay,
Between an Irish regiment an' English cavalree;
It started at Revelly an' it lasted on till dark:
The first man dropped at Harrison's, the last
    forninst the Park.
> For it was:—"Belts, belts, belts, an' that's
>   one for you!"   5
> An' it was "Belts, belts, belts, an' that's
>   done for you!"
> O buckle an' tongue
> Was the song that we sung
> From Harrison's down to the Park!

There was a row in Silver Street—the regiments
    was out,   10
They called us "Delhi Rebels,"° an' we answered
    "Threes about!"°
That drew them like a hornet's nest—we met
    them good an' large,
The English at the double an' the Irish at the
    charge.
> Then it was:—"Belts . . .

11 **Delhi Rebels** an English taunt of the Irish for supposed cowardice at the siege of Delhi during the Indian mutiny in 1857 **Threes about** This Irish retort refers to an incident at the battle of Chilianwala during the Sikh War in 1849 when an out-of-touch cavalry commander ordered his horsemen (drawn up in sections of threes) to retreat. Ever since, this officer's command, "Threes about," has been used to rile the two regiments involved—the 14th Hussars and the 9th Lancers.

There was a row in Silver Street—an' I was in
    it too;   *15*
We passed the time o' day, an' then the belts
    went whirraru!
I misremember what occurred, but subsequint
    the storm
A *Freeman's Journal Supplemint* was all my
    uniform.
        O it was:—"Belts . . .

There was a row in Silver Street—they sent the
    Polis there,   *20*
The English were too drunk to know, the Irish
    didn't care;
But when they grew impertinint we simultaneous
    rose,
Till half o' them was Liffey mud an' half was
    tatthered clo'es.
        For it was:—"Belts . . .

There was a row in Silver Street—it might ha'
    raged till now,   *25*
But some one drew his side-arm clear, an' nobody
    knew how;
'Twas Hogan took the point an' dropped; we saw
    the red blood run:
An' so we all was murderers that started out in
    fun.
        While it was:—"Belts . . .

There was a row in Silver Street—but that put
    down the shine,   *30*
Wid each man whisperin' to his next: " 'Twas
    never work o' mine!"
We went away like beaten dogs, an' down the
    street we bore him,
The poor dumb corpse that couldn't tell the bhoys
    were sorry for him.
        When it was:—"Belts . . .

There was a row in Silver Street—it isn't over yet,   35
For half of us are under guard wid punishments
    to get;
'Tis all a merricle to me as in the Clink I lie:
There was a row in Silver Street—begod, I
    wonder why!

      But it was:—"Belts, belts, belts, an' that's
        one for you!"
      An' it was "Belts, belts, belts, an' that's
        done for you!"   40
      O buckle an' tongue
      Was the song that we sung
      From Harrison's down to the Park!

      —*First published in* The Scots Observer
                  (26 July 1890)

The Young British Soldier

One of Kipling's most upbeat and heroic versions of the soldier's experience, this poem was frequently quoted—particularly the last stanza—in articles about the war in Afghanistan in 2002.

When the 'arf-made recruity goes out to the East
'E acts like a babe an' 'e drinks like a beast,
An' 'e wonders because 'e is frequent deceased
    Ere 'e's fit for to serve as a soldier.
      Serve, serve, serve as a soldier,   5
      Serve, serve, serve as a soldier,
      Serve, serve, serve as a soldier,
        So-oldier *OF* the Queen!

Now all you recruities what's drafted to-day,
You shut up your rag-box an' 'ark to my lay,   10
An' I'll sing you a soldier as far as I may:
    A soldier what's fit for a soldier.
      Fit, fit, fit for a soldier . . .

First mind you steer clear o' the grog-sellers' huts,
For they sell you Fixed Bay'nets° that rots out
    your guts—   15
Ay, drink that 'ud eat the live steel from your
    butts—
      An' it's bad for the young British soldier.
      Bad, bad, bad for the soldier . . .

When the cholera comes—as it will past a doubt—
Keep out of the wet and don't go on the shout,°   20
For the sickness gets in as the liquor dies out,
    An' it crumples the young British soldier.
      Crum-, crum-, crumples the soldier . . .

---

15 **Fixed Bay'nets** brandy or similar fiery spirits   20 **go on the shout** call for drinks (British colonial slang)

But the worst o' your foes is the sun over'ead:
You *must* wear your 'elmet for all that is said: *25*
If 'e finds you uncovered 'e'll knock you down
    dead,
      An' you'll die like a fool of a soldier.
        Fool, fool, fool of a soldier . . .

If you're cast for fatigue by a sergeant unkind,
Don't grouse like a woman nor crack on nor
    blind;°   *30*
Be handy and civil, and then you will find
      That it's beer for the young British soldier.
        Beer, beer, beer for the soldier . . .

Now, if you must marry, take care she is old—
A troop-sergeant's widow's the nicest I'm told,   *35*
For beauty won't help if your rations is cold,
      Nor love ain't enough for a soldier.
        'Nough, 'nough, 'nough for a soldier . . .

If the wife should go wrong with a comrade, be
    loath
To shoot when you catch 'em—you'll swing, on
    my oath!—   *40*
Make 'im take 'er and keep 'er: that's Hell for
    them both,
      An' you're shut o' the curse of a soldier.
        Curse, curse, curse of a soldier . . .

When first under fire an' you're wishful to duck,
Don't look nor take 'eed at the man that is struck,   *45*
Be thankful you're livin', and trust to your luck
      And march to your front like a soldier.
        Front, front, front like a soldier . . .

When 'arf of your bullets fly wide in the ditch,
Don't call your Martini° a cross-eyed old bitch;   *50*

---

30 **nor crack on nor blind** nor break down nor seem dim-
witted   50 **Martini** the Martini-Henry rifle

She's human as you are—you treat her as sich,
   An' she'll fight for the young British soldier.
      Fight, fight, fight for the soldier . . .

When shakin' their bustles like ladies so fine,
The guns o' the enemy wheel into line,   55
Shoot low at the limbers an' don't mind the shine,
   For noise never startles the soldier.
      Start-, start-, startles the soldier . . .

If your officer's dead and the sergeants look white,
Remember it's ruin to run from a fight: 60
So take open order, lie down, and sit tight,
   And wait for supports like a soldier.
      Wait, wait, wait like a soldier . . .

When you're wounded and left on Afghanistan's
   plains,
And the women come out to cut up what remains,   65
Jest roll to your rifle and blow out your brains
   An' go to your Gawd like a soldier.
     Go, go, go like a soldier,
     Go, go, go like a soldier,
     Go, go, go like a soldier,   70
      So-oldier *of* the Queen!

      —*First published in* The Scots Observer
                    (28 June 1890)

Mandalay

The most charming of the Barrack-Room Ballads, "Mandalay" evokes the nostalgia of the returned British squaddie for the Oriental world in which he has served. The clement weather, the attractive smells, the relaxed moral climate and, particularly, his cigar-chomping "Burma girl" provide fonder memories for the soldier than the realities of contemporary Britain. However, the geography of the piece is wayward: Moulmein, the Burmese port Kipling visited on his voyage eastward from Calcutta to San Francisco in 1889, had no "road to Mandalay" where "the old Flotilla lay." The sea is to the west rather than east of Moulmein, and India, rather than China, lies "crost the Bay."

By the old Moulmein Pagoda, lookin' eastward to
    the sea,
There's a Burma girl a-settin', and I know she
    thinks o' me;
For the wind is in the palm-trees, and the temple-
    bells they say:
"Come you back, you British soldier; come you
    back to Mandalay!"
        Come you back to Mandalay,   5
        Where the old Flotilla lay:
        Can't you 'ear their paddles chunkin' from
            Rangoon to Mandalay?
        On the road to Mandalay,
        Where the flyin'-fishes play,
        An' the dawn comes up like thunder outer
        China 'crost the Bay!   10

'Er petticoat was yaller an' 'er little cap was green,
An' 'er name was Supi-yaw-lat—jes' the same as
    Theebaw's Queen,°

12 **Supi-yaw-lat . . . Theebaw's Queen** title of the chief queen of King Tibaw, who ruled Burma during the Third Burmese war of 1885. (She was sometimes disparagingly referred to by the British troops as "Soup-plate.")

An' I seed her first a-smokin' of a whackin'
      white cheroot,
An' a-wastin' Christian kisses on an 'eathen
      idol's foot:
     Bloomin' idol made o'mud—   *15*
     Wot they called the Great Gawd Budd—°
     Plucky lot she cared for idols when I kissed
        'er where she stud!
     On the road to Mandalay . . .

When the mist was on the rice-fields an' the sun
      was droppin' slow,
She'd git 'er little banjo an' she'd sing "*Kulla-
      lo-lo!*"   *20*
With 'er arm upon my shoulder an' 'er cheek agin'
    my cheek
We useter watch the steamers an' the *hathis*°
    pilin' teak.
      Elephints a-pilin' teak
      In the sludgy, squdgy creek,
      Where the silence 'ung that 'eavy you
        was 'arf afraid to speak!   *25*
     On the road to Mandalay . . .

But that's all shove be'ind me—long ago an' fur
    away,
An' there ain't no 'busses runnin' from the Bank
    to Mandalay;
An' I'm learnin' 'ere in London what the ten-year
    soldier tells:
"If you've 'eard the East a-callin', you won't never
    'eed naught else."   *30*
     No! you won't 'eed nothin' else
     But them spicy garlic smells,
     An' the sunshine an' the palm-trees an'
      the tinkly temple-bells;
     On the road to Mandalay . . .

16 **Great Gawd Budd** Buddha 22 ***hathis*** Hindustani for
elephants

I am sick o' wastin' leather on these gritty
    pavin'-stones,   35
An' the blasted Henglish drizzle wakes the fever
    in my bones;
Tho' I walks with fifty 'ousemaids outer Chelsea
    to the Strand,
An' they talks a lot o' lovin', but wot do they
    understand?
        Beefy face an' grubby 'and—
        Law! wot do they understand?   40
        I've a neater, sweeter maiden in a cleaner,
            greener land!
        On the road to Mandalay . . .

Ship me somewheres east of Suez, where the best
    is like the worst,
Where there aren't no Ten Commandments an' a
    man can raise a thirst;
For the temple-bells are callin', an' it's there that
    I would be—   45
By the old Moulmein Pagoda, looking lazy at
    the sea;
        On the road to Mandalay,
        Where the old Flotilla lay,
        With our sick beneath the awnings when
            we went to Mandalay!
        On the road to Mandalay,   50
        Where the flyin'-fishes play,
        An' the dawn comes up like thunder outer
            China 'crost the Bay!

          —*First published in* The Scots Observer
                      (21 June 1890)

Troopin'

(Our Army in the East)

*A soldier who has served his allotted period of six years
in India is exhilarated as he is about to embark from
Bombay and return home in one of the troopships, the*
Malabar *or the* Jumna. *Even the realization that he will
arrive home in the depths of an English winter does
nothing to quell his joy.*

Troopin', troopin', troopin' to the sea:
'Ere's September come again—the six-year men
    are free.
O leave the dead be'ind us, for they cannot
    come away
To where the ship's a-coalin' up that takes us 'ome
    to-day.
        We're goin' 'ome, we're goin' 'ome,   5
          Our ship is at the shore,
        An' you must pack your 'aversack,
          For we won't come back no more.
        Ho, don't you grieve for me,
          My lovely Mary-Ann,   10
        For I'll marry you yit on a fourp'ny bit
          As a time-expired man.°

The *Malabar*'s in 'arbour with the *Jumner* at 'er
    tail,
An' the time-expired's waitin' of 'is orders for to
    sail.
Ho! the weary waitin' when on Khyber 'ills we lay,   15
But the time-expired's waitin' of 'is orders 'ome
    to-day.

11–12 **on a fourp'ny bit/As a time-expired man** A private who
served his six years abroad was transferred to the reserve,
where he received the none-too-generous retainer of four
pence a day.

They'll turn us out at Portsmouth wharf in cold
  an' wet an' rain,
All wearin' Injian cotton kit, but we will not
  complain;
They'll kill us of pneumonia—for that's their
  little way—
But damn the chills and fever, men, we're goin'
  'ome to-day!   20

Troopin', troopin', winter's round again!
See the new draf's pourin' in for the old campaign;
Ho, you poor recruities, but you've got to earn
  your pay—
What's the last from Lunnon, lads? We're goin'
  there to-day.

Troopin', troopin', give another cheer—   25
'Ere's to English women an' a quart of English
  beer.
The Colonel an' the regiment an' all who've got
  to stay,
Gawd's mercy strike 'em gentle—Whoop! we're
  goin' 'ome to-day.
        We're goin' 'ome, we're goin' 'ome,
          Our ship is at the shore,   30
        An' you must pack your 'aversack,
          For we won't come back no more.
        Ho, don't you grieve for me,
          My lovely Mary-Ann,
        For I'll marry you yit on a fourp'ny bit   35
          As a time-expired man.

          —*First published in* The Scots Observer
                      (17 May 1890)

The Widow's Party

This is another take on the experience of the British soldier serving the "Widow" (Queen Victoria) abroad. The food may be awful, but at the end of the day, he and his colleagues have conquered, bringing justice, communications and sanitation to a country where once there was none. This is a cynical but ultimately triumphalist version of the imperialist project, as well as a realistic portrayal of the way the common soldier regarded his responsibilities.

"Where have you been this while away,
        Johnnie, Johnnie?"
'Long with the rest on a picnic lay,
        Johnnie, my Johnnie, aha!
They called us out of the barrack-yard   5
To Gawd knows where from Gosport Hard,°
And you can't refuse when you get the card,
        And the Widow give the party.
           (*Bugle*: Ta—rara—ra-ra-rara!)

"What did you get to eat and drink,   10
        Johnnie, Johnnie?"
Standing water as thick as ink,
        Johnnie, my Johnnie, aha!
A bit o' beef that were three year stored,
A bit o' mutton as tough as a board,   15
And a fowl we killed with a sergeant's sword,
        When the Widow give the party.

"What did you do for knives and forks,
        Johnnie, Johnnie?"
We carries 'em with us wherever we walks,   20
        Johnnie, my Johnnie, aha!
And some was sliced and some was halved,
And some was crimped and some was carved,

6 **Gosport Hard** the dock at Portsmouth from which troopships
sailed to India

And some was gutted and some was starved,
        When the Widow give the party.   25

"What ha' you done with half your mess,
        Johnnie, Johnnie?"
They couldn't do more and they wouldn't do less,
        Johnnie, my Johnnie, aha!
They ate their whack and they drank their fill,   30
And I think the rations has made them ill,
For half my comp'ny's lying still
        Where the Widow give the party.

"How did you get away—away,
        Johnnie, Johnnie?"   35
On the broad o' my back at the end o' the day,
        Johnnie, my Johnnie, aha!
I comed away like a bleedin' toff,
For I got four niggers to carry me off,
As I lay in the bight of a canvas trough,   40
        When the Widow give the party.

"What was the end of all the show,
        Johnnie, Johnnie?"
Ask my Colonel, for *I* don't know,
        Johnnie, my Johnnie, aha!   45
We broke a King and we built a road—
A court-house stands where the reg'ment goed.
And the river's clean where the raw blood flowed
        When the Widow give the party.
          (*Bugle*: Ta—rara—ra-ra-rara!)   50

—First published in The National Observer
        (22 November 1890)

Ford o' Kabul River

This poem recalls an incident in the Second Afghan War (1878–80) when the 10th Hussars tried to ford the Kabul River on the night of 31 March 1879. They were surprised by a flash flood that killed one officer, forty-six men and fourteen horses.

Kabul town's by Kabul river—
    Blow the bugle,° draw the sword—
There I lef' my mate for ever,
    Wet an' drippin' by the ford.
        Ford, ford, ford o' Kabul river,   5
            Ford o' Kabul river in the dark!
        There's the river up and brimmin', an'
            there's 'arf a squadron swimmin'
            'Cross the ford o' Kabul river in
            the dark.

Kabul town's a blasted place—
    Blow the bugle, draw the sword—   10
'Strewth I sha'n't forget 'is face
    Wet an' drippin' by the ford!
        Ford, ford, ford o' Kabul river,
            Ford o' Kabul river in the dark!
        Keep the crossing-stakes beside you, an'
            they will surely guide you   15
            'Cross the ford o' Kabul river in the
            dark.

Kabul town is sun and dust—
    Blow the bugle, draw the sword—
I'd ha' sooner drownded fust
    'Stead of 'im beside the ford.   20
        Ford, ford, ford o' Kabul river,

2 **Blow the bugle** In later editions the bugle was changed to a trumpet. The former is used inside barracks to sound regular calls such as reveille (time to get up); the latter is used by cavalry to convey orders in the field, above the sound of battle.

Ford o' Kabul river in the dark!
You can 'ear the 'orses threshin', you can
'ear the men a-splashin',
'Cross the ford o' Kabul river in the
dark.

Kabul town was ours to take—   25
    Blow the bugle, draw the sword—
I'd ha' left it for 'is sake—
    'Im that left me by the ford.
        Ford, ford, ford o' Kabul river,
            Ford o' Kabul river in the dark!   30
        It's none so bloomin' dry there; ain't you
            never comin' nigh there,
                'Cross the ford o' Kabul river in the
                dark?

Kabul town'll go to hell—
    Blow the bugle, draw the sword—
'Fore I see him 'live an' well—   35
    'Im the best beside the ford.
        Ford, ford, ford o' Kabul river,
            Ford o' Kabul river in the dark!
        Gawd 'elp 'em if they blunder, for their
            boots'll pull 'em under,
                By the ford o' Kabul river in the dark.   40

Turn your 'orse from Kabul town—
    Blow the bugle, draw the sword—
'Im an' 'arf my troop is down,
    Down an' drownded by the ford.
        Ford, ford, ford o' Kabul river,   45
            Ford o' Kabul river in the dark!
        There's the river low an' fallin', but it
            ain't no use o' callin'
                'Cross the ford o' Kabul river in
                the dark.

—*First published in* The National Observer
                    (22 November 1890)

Gentlemen-Rankers

*Here Kipling assumes the perspective of a different
kind of soldier, the gentleman-ranker: a member of the
gentry who for one reason or another (often because
he is the "black sheep" of his family) is forced or
decides of his own volition to join the army in the ranks
rather than as an officer.*

To the legion of the lost ones, to the cohort of
      the damned,
    To my brethren in their sorrow overseas,
Sings a gentleman of England cleanly bred,
      machinely crammed,
    And a trooper of the Empress, if you please.
Yea, a trooper of the forces who has run his own
      six horses,   5
    And faith he went the pace and went it blind,
And the world was more than kin while he held
      the ready tin,
    But to-day the Sergeant's something less than
      kind.
           We're poor little lambs° who've lost
              our way,
                Baa! Baa! Baa!   10
           We're little black sheep who've
              gone astray,
                Baa—aa—aa!
           Gentlemen-rankers out on the spree,
           Damned from here to Eternity,
           God ha' mercy on such as we,   15
                Baa! Yah! Bah!

Oh, it's sweet to sweat through stables, sweet to
      empty kitchen slops,

9 **We're poor little lambs . . .** This refrain was borrowed for
"The Whiffenpoof Song," anthem of the famous Yale singing
group, with the substitution of "gentlemen-songsters" for
"gentlemen-rankers."

And it's sweet to hear the tales the troopers
tell,
To dance with blowzy housemaids at the
regimental hops
And thrash the cad who says you waltz too
well.   20
Yes, it makes you cock-a-hoop° to be "Rider" to
your troop,°
And branded with a blasted worsted spur,
When you envy, O how keenly, one poor Tommy
being cleanly
Who blacks your boots and sometimes calls
you "Sir."

If the home we never write to, and the oaths we
never keep,   25
And all we know most distant and most dear,
Across the snoring barrack-room return to break
our sleep,
Can you blame us if we soak ourselves in
beer?
When the drunken comrade mutters and the great
guard-lantern gutters
And the horror of our fall is written plain,   30
Every secret, self-revealing on the aching white-
washed ceiling,
Do you wonder that we drug ourselves from
pain?

We have done with Hope and Honour, we are
lost to Love and Truth,
We are dropping down the ladder rung by
rung,
And the measure of our torment is the measure
of our youth.   35

21 **cock-a-hoop** exultant, proud   **to be "Rider" to your troop**
The roughrider was a noncommissioned officer who trained
and looked after young horses. His badge was a spur that he
wore in his worsted uniform. (See next line.)

50

God help us, for we knew the worst too young!
Our shame is clean repentance for the crime that
    brought the sentence,
Our pride it is to know no spur of pride,
And the Curse of Reuben° holds us till an alien
    turf enfolds us
And we die, and none can tell Them where
    we died. ·   *40*
           We're poor little lambs who've lost our
               way,
                 Baa! Baa! Baa!
           We're little black sheep who've gone
               astray,
                 Baa—aa—aa!
           Gentlemen-rankers out on the spree,   *45*
           Damned from here to Eternity,
           God ha' mercy on such as we,
                 Baa! Yah! Bah!

—*First published in* Barrack-Room Ballads and
                Other Verses *(London, 1892)*

---

39 the Curse of Reuben 1 Chronicles 5:1 states that the birthright
of the sons of Reuben, "the firstborn of Israel," was given
instead to the sons of Joseph after Reuben defiled his
father's bed.

Route Marchin'

This marching song recalls the soldier's experience of tramping up and down the Grand Trunk Road, which crosses Northern India from Peshawar to Calcutta. Normally the road was teeming with people, moving from village to village or going on a long journey. The exploits and energy of these ordinary folk on the Grand Trunk Road provide a memorable feature of Kipling's 1901 novel, Kim.

We're marchin' on relief over Injia's sunny plains,
A little front o' Christmas-time an' just be'ind
    the Rains;
Ho! get away you bullock-man, you've 'eard the
    bugle blowed,
There's a regiment a-comin' down the Grand
    Trunk Road;
      With its best foot first   5
      And the road a-sliding past,
      An' every bloomin' campin'-ground exactly
        like the last;
      While the Big Drum says,
      With 'is *"rowdy-dowdy-dow!"* —
      "Kiko kissywarsti don't you *hamsher argy*
        jow?"°   10

Oh, there's them Injian temples to admire when
    you see,
There's the peacock round the corner an' the
    monkey up the tree,
An' there's that rummy silver grass a-wavin' in
    the wind,
An' the old Grand Trunk a-trailin' like a rifle-
    sling be'ind.
      While it's best foot first, . . .   15

10 *Kiko kissywarsti* **don't you** *hamsher argy jow?* Kipling
translates this freely as "Why don't you get on?"

At half-past five's Revelly, an' our tents they
    down must come,
Like a lot of button mushrooms when you pick
    'em up at 'ome.
But it's over in a minute, an' at six the column
    starts,
While the women and the kiddies sit an' shiver in
    the carts.
        An' it's best foot first, . . .   *20*

Oh, then it's open order, an' we lights our pipes
    an' sings,
An' we talks about our rations an' a lot of other
    things,
An' we thinks o' friends in England, an' we
    wonders what they're at,
An' 'ow they would admire for to hear us sling
    the *bat.*°
        An' it's best foot first, . . .   *25*

It's none so bad o' Sunday, when you're lyin' at
    your ease,
To watch the kites a-wheelin' round them feather-
    'eaded trees,
For although there ain't no women, yet there ain't
    no barrick-yards,
So the orficers goes shootin' an' the men they
    plays at cards.
        Till it's best foot first, . . .   *30*

So 'ark an' 'eed, you rookies, which is always
    grumblin' sore,
There's worser things than marchin' from Umballa
    to Cawnpore;°

24 **sling the *bat*** speak the local language. While Tommy may
have fancied himself a profound Orientalist and fluent speaker
of Hindustani, the typical soldier usually got by with sign
language. 32 **Umballa to Cawnpore** a five-hundred-mile
march, supposed to take four weeks

53

An' if your 'eels are blistered an' they feels to 'urt
    like 'ell,
You drop some tallow in your socks an' that will
    make 'em well.
       For it's best foot first, . . .   35

We're marchin' on relief over Injia's coral strand,
Eight 'undred fightin' Englishmen, the Colonel,
    and the Band;
Ho! get away you bullock-man, you've 'eard the
    bugle blowed,
There's a regiment a-comin' down the Grand
    Trunk Road;
      With its best foot first   40
      And the road a-sliding past,
      An' every bloomin' campin'-ground exactly
        like the last;
      While the Big Drum says,
      With 'is "*rowdy-dowdy-dow!*" —
      "*Kiko kissywarsti* don't you *hamsher argy*
        jow?"
                          45

—*First published in* Barrack-Room Ballads and
          Other Verses *(London, 1892)*

Shillin' a Day

A rousing anthem, based on an old Cockney song, which highlights the role of the Irish in the British army. Kipling, who was part Irish on his mother's side, was in his later years a vehement opponent of Irish home rule. However, he had great respect for the resilience and humor of the Irish fighting man. His son John served with the Irish Guards in World War I and was killed at the Battle of Loos in 1915. Kipling later wrote a two-volume History of the Irish Guards.

My name is O'Kelly, I've heard the Revelly
From Birr to Bareilly,° from Leeds to Lahore,
Hong-Kong and Peshawur,
Lucknow and Etawah,
And fifty-five more all endin' in "pore."   5
Black Death and his quickness, the depth and
    the thickness,
Of sorrow and sickness I've known on my way,
But I'm old and I'm nervis,
I'm cast from the Service,
And all I deserve is a shillin' a day.   10
    (*Chorus*) Shillin' a day,
            Bloomin' good pay—
            Lucky to touch it, a shillin' a day!

Oh, it drives me half crazy to think of the days I
Went slap for the Ghazi,° my sword at my side,   15
When we rode Hell-for-leather
Both squadrons together,
That didn't care whether we lived or we died.
But it's no use despairin', my wife must go
    charin'°

2 **Birr to Bareilly** Birr is a town in County Offaly, Ireland; Bareilly a town in Uttar Pradesh, India. 15 **Went slap for the Ghazi** marched or rode straight into the Ghazi, Moslem fanatics 19 **charin'** housecleaning

An' me commissairin' the pay-bills to better,°   20
So if me you be'old
In the wet and the cold,
By the Grand Metropold,° won't you give me a
    letter?
(*Full chorus*) Give 'im a letter—
        'Can't do no better,   25
        Late Troop-Sergeant-Major an'—
           runs with a letter!
        Think what 'e's been,
        Think what 'e's seen,
        Think of his pension an'——
           GAWD SAVE THE QUEEN.   30

    —*First published in* Barrack-Room Ballads and
           Other Verses (*London, 1892*)

---

20 commissairin' the pay-bills to better work as a commissionaire, or hotel doorman, to earn extra money. This was a job often taken by retired soldiers and the profession was run in a quasimilitary fashion   **23 Grand Metropold** the Grand Metropole, here used as a generic name for a hotel

Prelude

Not strictly a Barrack-Room Ballad, this was a typically Kiplingesque reflection on the way that all artists copy those who have gone before. It was apposite that he should use it as a prelude to the Barrack-Room Ballads section of The Seven Seas, *as this type of soldier's song inevitably drew on much that had gone before it.*

When 'Omer smote 'is bloomin' lyre,
  He'd 'eard men sing by land an' sea;
An' what he thought 'e might require,
  'E went an' took—the same as me!

The market-girls an' fishermen,   5
  The shepherds an' the sailors, too,
They 'eard old songs turn up again,
  But kep' it quiet—same as you!

They knew 'e stole; 'e knew they knowed.
  They didn't tell, nor make a fuss,   10
But winked at 'Omer down the road,
  An' 'e winked back—the same as us!

      —First published in The Seven Seas
       (London and New York, 1896)

"Back to the Army Again"

The first full poem of the second series of Barrack-Room Ballads; the title and subject matter reflect Kipling's return to his military theme. The speaker of the poem, a soldier who has done his six years' service and retired to the reserves (see "Troopin' "), finds he cannot make it in civilian life. Because he is overage, he reenlists under a new name, and the drill sergeant and sergeant-tailor do not let on they know. This humorous poem shows how an individual is shaped by and often cannot throw off the institutional life of the army.

I'm 'ere in a ticky ulster° an' a broken billycock
    'at,
A-layin' on to the sergeant I don't know a gun
    from a bat;
My shirt's doin' duty for jacket, my sock's stickin'
    out o' my boots,
An' I'm learnin' the damned old goose-step along
    o' the new recruits!

        Back to the Army again, sergeant,   5
        Back to the Army again.
      Don't look so 'ard, for I 'aven't no card,°
      I'm back to the Army again!

I done my six years' service. 'Er Majesty sez:
    "Good-day—
You'll please to come when you're rung for, an'
    'ere's your 'ole back-pay;   10
An' fourpence a day for baccy—an' bloomin'
    gen'rous, too;
An' now you can make your fortune—the same
    as your orf'cers do."

1 **ticky ulster** overcoat infested with lice   7 **'aven't no card** haven't got discharge papers

Back to the Army again, sergeant,
Back to the Army again;
'Ow did I learn to do right-about turn?   *15*
I'm back to the Army again!

A man o' four-an'-twenty that 'asn't learned of
    a trade—
Beside "Reserve" agin' him—'e'd better be
    never made.
I tried my luck for a quarter, an' that was enough
    for me,
An' I thought of 'Er Majesty's barricks, an' I
    thought I'd go an' see.   *20*

Back to the Army again, sergeant,
Back to the Army again;
'Tisn't my fault if I dress when I 'alt—°
I'm back to the Army again!

The sergeant arst no questions, but 'e winked the
    other eye,   *25*
'E sez to me, " 'Shun!" an' I shunted, the same
    as in days gone by;
For 'e saw the set o' my shoulders, an' I couldn't
    'elp 'oldin' straight
When me an' the other rookies come under the
    barrick-gate.

Back to the Army again, sergeant,
Back to the Army again;   *30*
'Oo would ha' thought I could carry an' port?
I'm back to the Army again!

I took my bath, an' I wallered—for, Gawd, I
    needed it so!
I smelt the smell o' the barricks, I 'eard the
    bugles go.

23 **dress when I 'alt** In military terms, to dress means to get
into proper alignment (as in a parade).

I 'eard the feet on the gravel—the feet o' the men
    what drill—   35
An' I sez to my flutterin' 'eart-strings, I sez to
    'em, "Peace, be still!"

      Back to the Army again, sergeant,
        Back to the Army again;
    'Oo said I knew when the *Jumner*° was due?
    I'm back to the Army again!   40

I carried my slops to the tailor; I sez to 'im, "None
    o' your lip!
You tight 'em over the shoulders, an' loose 'em
    over the 'ip,
For the set o' the tunic's 'orrid." An' 'e sez to
    me, "Strike me dead,
But I thought you was used to the business!" an'
    so 'e done what I said.

      Back to the Army again, sergeant,   45
        Back to the Army again.
      Rather too free with my fancies? Wot—me?
    I'm back to the Army again!

Next week I'll 'ave 'em fitted; I'll buy me a
    swagger-cane;°
They'll let me free o' the barricks to walk on the
    Hoe° again   50
In the name o' William Parsons, that used to be
    Edward Clay,
An'—any pore beggar that wants it can draw my
    fourpence a day!

      Back to the Army again, sergeant,
        Back to the Army again:
      Out o' the cold an' the rain, sergeant,   55
      Out o' the cold an' the rain.

39 *Jumner* name of a troopship   49 **swagger-cane** a short stick
soldiers carried when outside the barracks   50 **the Hoe** the
promontory off the port of Plymouth

"Back to the Army Again"

'Oo's there?

A man that's too good to be lost you,
    A man that is 'andled an' made—
A man that will pay what 'e cost you   *60*
    In learnin' the others their trade—
        parade!
You're droppin' the pick o' the Army
    Because you don't 'elp 'em remain,
But drives 'em to cheat to get out o'
    the street
    An' back to the Army again!   *65*

—First published in Pall Mall Gazette *(August 1894)*

"Birds of Prey" March

This song depicts draftees marching through the rain on their way to the troopship that will carry them to service overseas. As in many military songs, the chorus is pessimistic, as if verbalizing the worst outcome somehow can protect against its happening.

March! The mud is cakin' good about our trousies.
    Front!—eyes front, an' watch the Colour-
        casin's drip.
Front! The faces of the women in the 'ouses
    Ain't the kind o' things to take aboard the
        ship.

      Cheer! An' we'll never march to victory.   5
      Cheer! An' we'll never live to 'ear the
        cannon roar!
        The Large Birds o' Prey
        They will carry us away,
      An' you'll never see your soldiers any
        more!

Wheel! Oh, keep your touch; we're goin' round
    a corner.   10
      Time!—mark time, an' let the men be'ind
        us close.
Lord! the transport's full, an' 'alf our lot not on
    'er—
      Cheer, O cheer! We're going off where no
        one knows.

March! The Devil's none so black as 'e is painted!
    Cheer! We'll 'ave some fun before we're
        put away.   15
'Alt, an' 'and 'er out—a woman's gone and
    fainted!
      Cheer! Get on—Gawd 'elp the married men
        to-day!

Hoi! Come up, you 'ungry beggars, to yer sorrow.
    ('Ear them say they want their tea, an' want
        it quick!)
You won't have no mind for slingers,° not to-
    morrow—   20
    No; you'll put the 'tween-decks stove out,
        bein' sick!

'Alt! The married kit 'as all to go before us!
    'Course it's blocked the bloomin' gangway
        up again!
Cheer, O cheer the 'Orse Guards watchin' tender
    o'er us,
    Keepin' us since eight this mornin' in the   25
        rain!

Stuck in 'eavy marchin'-order, sopped and
    wringin'—
    Sick, before our time to watch 'er 'eave
        an' fall,
'Ere's your 'appy 'ome at last, an' stop your
    singin'.
    'Alt! Fall in along the troop-deck! Silence
    all!

    Cheer! For we'll never live to see no
        bloomin' victory!   30
    Cheer! An' we'll never live to 'ear the
        cannon roar! (One cheer more!)
    The jackal an' the kite
    'Ave an 'ealthy appetite,
    An' you'll never see your soldiers any
        more! ('Ip! Urroar!)
    The eagle an' the crow   35
    They are waitin' ever so,
    An' you'll never see your soldiers any
        more! ('Ip! Urroar!)
    Yes, the Large Birds o' Prey

20 **slingers** pieces of bread dipped in tea (army slang)

They will carry us away,
An' you'll never see your soldiers any
                    more!   40

—First published in Pall Mall Gazette *(30 May 1895)*

"Soldier an' Sailor Too"

A backhanded paean to the Royal Marines, who are a cross between a soldier and a sailor—"a kind of a giddy harumfrodite," says the narrator in one of several malapropisms.

As I was spittin' into the Ditch° aboard o' the
    Crocodile,
I seed a man on a man-o'-war got up in the
    Reg'lars' style.
'E was scrapin' the paint from off of 'er plates,
    an' I sez to 'im, " 'Oo are you?"
Sez 'e, "I'm a Jolly°—'Er Majesty's Jolly—soldier
    an' sailor too!"
Now 'is work begins by Gawd knows when, and
    'is work is never through;   5
'E isn't one o' the reg'lar Line, nor 'e isn't one of
    the crew.
'E's a kind of a giddy harumfrodite—soldier an'
    sailor too!

An' after I met 'im all over the world, a-doin' all
    kinds of things,
Like landin' 'isself with a Gatlin' gun to talk to
    them 'eathen kings;
'E sleeps in an 'ammick instead of a cot, an' 'e
    drills with the deck on a slew,   10
An' 'e sweats like a Jolly—'Er Majesty's Jolly—
    soldier an' sailor too!
For there isn't a job on the top o' the earth the
    beggar don't know, nor do—
You can leave 'im at night on a bald man's 'ead,
    to paddle 'is own canoe—
'E's a sort of a bloomin' cosmopolouse—soldier
    an' sailor too.

1 **the Ditch** the Suez Canal   4 **Jolly** Royal Marine

We've fought 'em in trooper, we've fought 'em in
    dock, and drunk with 'em in betweens,   15
When they called us the seasick scull'ry-maids, an'
    we called 'em the Ass Marines;
But, when we was down for a double fatigue, from
    Woolwich to Bernardmyo,°
We sent for the Jollies—'Er Majesty's Jollies—
    soldier an' sailor too!
They think for 'emselves, an' they steal for
    'emselves, and they never ask what's to do,
But they're camped an' fed an' they're up an' fed
    before our bugle's blew.   20
Ho! they ain't no limpin' procrastitutes—soldier
    an' sailor too.

You may say we are fond of an 'arness-cut,° or
    'ootin' in barrick-yards,
Or startin' a Board School mutiny° along o' the
    Onion Guards;°
But once in a while we can finish in style for the
    ends of the earth to view,
The same as the Jollies—'Er Majesty's Jollies—
    soldier an' sailor too!   25
They come of our lot, they was brothers to us;
    they was beggars we'd met an' knew;
Yes, barrin' an inch in the chest an' the arm, they
    was doubles o' me an' you;
For they weren't no special chrysanthemums—
    soldier an' sailor too!

17 from Woolwich to Bernardmyo Woolwich, in southeast
London, was the headquarters of a Royal Marines barracks and
home of the Royal Military Academy. Bernardmyo is a town in
Burma.   **22 an 'arness-cut** To harness-cut is to draw attention
to one's grievances (also achieved by " 'ootin' in the barrick-
yards").   **23 Board School mutiny** Board schools were free schools
run by the Board of Education. Here it means a childish
rebellion.   **Onion Guards** the second battalion of the Grenadier
Guards, who, having refused to parade in their Wellington
Barracks in London in 1890, were sent to Bermuda, then seen as a
punishment station. Onions were the island's staple crop.

To take your chance in the thick of a rush, with
    firing all about,
Is nothing so bad when you've cover to 'and, an'
    leave an' likin' to shout;   30
But to stand an' be still to the *Birken'ead* drill° is
    a damn tough bullet to chew,
An' they done it, the Jollies—'Er Majesty's
    Jollies—soldier an' sailor too!
Their work was done when it 'adn't begun; they
    was younger nor me an' you;
Their choice it was plain between drownin' in
    'eaps an' bein' mopped by the screw,°
So they stood an' was still to the *Birken'ead* drill,
    soldier an' sailor too!   35

We're most of us liars, we're 'arf of us thieves,
    an' the rest are as rank as can be,
But once in a while we can finish in style (which
    I 'ope it won't 'appen to me).
But it makes you think better o' you an' your
    friends, an' the work you may 'ave to do,
When you think o' the sinkin' *Victorier*'s Jollies°—
    soldier an' sailor too!
Now there isn't no room for to say ye don't
    know—they 'ave proved it plain and true—   40
That whether it's Widow, or whether it's ship,°
    Victorier's work is to do,
An' they done it, the Jollies—'Er Majesty's
    Jollies—soldier an' sailor too!

—*First published in* Pearson's Magazine *(April 1896)*

31 **the *Birken'ead* drill** A detachment of Marines maintained
discipline and stood to arms on deck as the troopship the
Birkenhead went down off Cape Town in 1852. 34 **mopped
by the screw** absorbed and therefore killed by the ship's screw-
propellor 39 **the sinkin' *Victorier*'s Jollies** a similar act of
bravery by the Marines when they tried to close the bulkhead
doors after the battleship *Victoria* was rammed off Syria in
June 1893 and commenced to sink 41 **Whether it's Widow,
or whether it's ship** whether the army or the navy

Sappers

*The Sappers are the Royal Engineers. Though poking
gentle fun at the superior attitude of the Sappers, the
poem nevertheless makes clear how greatly the army
relied on its builders and engineers. Kipling had great
personal regard for engineers as men of action who
made a difference. They were the people whose hard
work allowed the colonialists to bring the fruits of civi-
lization to the world.*

When the Waters were dried an' the Earth did
    appear,
    ("It's all one," says the Sapper),
The Lord He created the Engineer,
    Her Majesty's Royal Engineer,
    With the rank and pay of a Sapper!   *5*

When the Flood come along for an extra
    monsoon,
'Twas Noah constructed the first pontoon
    To the plans of Her Majesty's, etc.

But after fatigue in the wet an' the sun,
Old Noah got drunk, which he wouldn't ha' done *10*
    If he'd trained with, etc.

When the Tower o' Babel had mixed up men's
    bat,°
Some clever civilian was managing that,
    An' none of, etc.

When the Jews had a fight at the foot of a hill, *15*
Young Joshua ordered the sun to stand still,
    For he was a Captain of Engineers, etc.

When the Children of Israel made bricks
    without straw,

12 *bat* language (Hindustani)

They were learnin' the regular work of our Corps, 20
   The work of, etc.

For ever since then, if a war they would wage,
Behold us a-shinin' on history's page—
   First page for, etc.

We lay down their sidings an' help 'em entrain,
An' we sweep up their mess through the
    bloomin' campaign, 25
   In the style of, etc.

They send us in front with a fuse an' a mine
To blow up the gates that are rushed by the Line,
   But bent by, etc.

They send us behind with a pick an' a spade, 30
To dig for the guns of a bullock-brigade
   Which has asked for, etc.

We work under escort in trousers and shirt,
An' the heathen they plug us tail-up in the dirt,
   Annoying, etc. 35

We blast out the rock an' we shovel the mud,
We make 'em good roads an'—they roll down
    the *khud*,°
   Reporting, etc.

We make 'em their bridges, their wells, an' their
   huts,
An' the telegraph-wire the enemy cuts, 40
   An' it's blamed on, etc.

An' when we return, an' from war we would
   cease,
They grudge us adornin' the billets of peace,
   Which are kept for, etc.

37 *khud* ravine (Hindustani)

We build 'em nice barracks—they swear they
    are bad,   45
That our Colonels are Methodist, married or mad,
    Insultin', etc.

They haven't no manners nor gratitude too,
For the more that we help 'em, the less will
    they do,
    But mock at, etc.   50

Now the Line's but a man with a gun in his hand,
An' Cavalry's only what horses can stand,
    When helped by, etc.

Artillery moves by the leave o' the ground,
But *we* are the men that do something all round,   55
    For *we* are, etc.

I have stated it plain, an' my argument's thus
    ("It's all one," says the Sapper),
There's only one Corps which is perfect—that's
    us;
    An' they call us Her Majesty's Engineers,   60
    Her Majesty's Royal Engineers,
    With the rank and pay of a Sapper!

        —*First published in* Pall Mall Gazette
                (25 April 1895)

That Day

*This poem recalls the routing of a mixed brigade of
British and Indian troops under General Burrows at
Maiwand in July 1880, toward the end of the Second
Afghan War. Of the 2,476 men who fought at
Maiwand, nearly a thousand were killed. Their fate led
to General (later Lord) Frederick Roberts's famous
march from Kabul to Kandahar in which he avenged
the earlier defeat.*

It got beyond all orders an' it got beyond all 'ope;
  It got to shammin' wounded an' retirin' from
    the 'alt.
'Ole companies was lookin' for the nearest road
    to slope;
  It were just a bloomin' knock-out—an' our
    fault!

    Now there ain't no chorus 'ere to give,   5
      Nor there ain't no band to play;
    An' I wish I was dead 'fore I done what
      I did,
      Or seen what I seed that day!

We was sick o' bein' punished, an' we let 'em
    know it, too;
  An' a company-commander up an' 'it us with
    a sword,   10
An' some one shouted " 'Ook it!" an' it come to
    sove-ki-poo,°
An' we chucked our rifles from us—O my
    Gawd!

There was thirty dead an' wounded on the ground
    we wouldn't keep—

11 **sove-ki-poo** *sauve qui peut* or save yourself if you can

71

No, there wasn't more than twenty when the
    front begun to go;
But, Christ! along the line o' flight they cut us up
    like sheep,   *15*
    An' that was all we gained by doin' so.

I 'eard the knives be'ind me, but I dursn't face
    my man,
    Nor I don't know where I went to, 'cause I
        didn't 'alt to see,
Till I 'eard a beggar squealin' out for quarter as
    'e ran,
    An' I thought I knew the voice an'—it was me! *20*

We was 'idin' under bedsteads more than 'arf a
    march away;
    We was lyin' up like rabbits all about the
        countryside;
An' the major cursed 'is Maker 'cause 'e lived to
    see that day,
    An' the colonel broke 'is sword acrost, an' cried.

We was rotten 'fore we started—we was never
    disci*plined*;   *25*
    We made it out a favour if an order was obeyed;
Yes, every little drummer 'ad 'is rights an' wrongs
    to mind,
    So we had to pay for teachin'—an' we paid!

The papers 'id it 'andsome, but you know the
    Army knows;
    We was put to groomin' camels till the
        regiments withdrew,   *30*
An' they gave us each a medal for subduin'
    England's foes,
    An' I 'ope you like my song—because it's true!

    An' there ain't no chorus 'ere to give,
        Nor there ain't no band to play;

That Day

But I wish I was dead 'fore I done what
   I did,
Or seen what I seed that day!

—First published in Pall Mall Gazette
(25 April 1895)

35

"The Men That Fought at Minden"

A Song of Instruction

This is a soldier's humorous, rose-tinted recollection of one of the past successes of the British army—when a British brigade (including soldiers from the 5th [Northumberland Fusiliers], a regiment that Kipling had come to know in Lahore) helped an Allied force under Prince Ferdinand of Brunswick defeat the French at the battle of Minden in Germany on 1 August 1759. The brigade was reputed to have fought in a rose garden, a circumstance whose anniversary was commemorated each year by its member regiments going on parade with a rose in their caps. The ballad subtly examines the way older soldiers wield their power over young recruits ("Johnny Raw") in the guise of offering wise counsel.

The men that fought at Minden, they was rookies
    in their time—
  So was them that fought at Waterloo!
All the 'ole command, yuss, from Minden to
    Maiwand,
  They was once dam' sweeps like you!

    Then do not be discouraged, 'Eaven is your
      'elper,   5
      We'll learn you not to forget;
    An' you mustn't swear an' curse, or you'll
      only catch it worse,
      For we'll make you soldiers yet!

The men that fought at Minden, they 'ad stocks°
    beneath their chins,
  Six inch 'igh an' more;   10
But fatigue it was their pride, and they *would* not
    be denied

9 **stocks** stiff collars, originally used by clergy

To clean the cook-'ouse floor.

The men that fought at Minden, they had
  anarchistic bombs
 Served to 'em by name of 'and-grenades;
But they got it in the eye (same as you will by-
  an'-by)   *15*
 When they clubbed their field-parades.°

The men that fought at Minden, they 'ad buttons
  up an' down,
 Two-an'-twenty dozen of 'em told;
But they didn't grouse an' shirk at an hour's
  extry work,
 They kept 'em bright as gold.   *20*

The men that fought at Minden, they was armed
  with musketoons,
 Also, they was drilled by 'alberdiers;°
I don't know what they were, but the sergeants
  took good care
 They washed be'ind their ears.

The men that fought at Minden, they 'ad ever cash
  in 'and   *25*
 Which they did not bank nor save,
But spent it gay an' free on their betters—such
  as me—
 For the good advice I gave.

The men that fought at Minden, they was civil—
  yuss, they was—
 Never didn't talk o' rights an' wrongs, *30*
But they got it with the toe (same as you will get
  it—so!)—
 For interrupting songs.

16 **clubbed their field parades** became bunched up or out of
line in a parade (as after performing a wheel or other maneuver)
22 **'alberdiers** A halberd was a weapon used in the late Middle
Ages, a combination of a spear and battle-ax, mounted on a
handle five or seven feet long.

The men that fought at Minden, they was several
  other things
 Which I don't remember clear;
But *that's* the reason why, now the six-year men
  are dry,   35
 The rooks will stand the beer!

 Then do not be discouraged, 'Eaven is your
   'elper,
  We'll learn you not to forget;
 An' you mustn't swear an' curse, or you'll only
   catch it worse,
  For we'll make you soldiers yet!   40

 Soldiers yet, if you've got it in you—
  All for the sake of the Core;
 Soldiers yet, if we 'ave to skin you—
  Run an' get the beer, Johnny Raw—
   Johnny Raw!
  Ho! run an' get the beer, Johnny Raw!   45

—*First published in* Pall Mall Gazette *(9 May 1895)*

Cholera Camp

A grim reminder of the terrible toll taken by cholera among British troops in India, particularly in the hot monsoon months of late summer.

We've got the cholerer in camp—it's worse than
    forty fights;
We're dyin' in the wilderness the same as Isrulites;
It's before us, an' be'ind us, an' we cannot get
    away,
An' the doctor's just reported we've ten more
    to-day!

    Oh, strike your camp an' go, the Bugle's
      callin',   5
      The Rains are fallin'—
    The dead are bushed an' stoned° to keep 'em
      safe below;
    The Band's a-doin' all she knows to cheer us;
    The Chaplain's gone and prayed to Gawd to
      'ear us—
      To 'ear us—   10
    O Lord, for it's a-killin' of us so!

Since August, when it started, it's been stickin' to
    our tail,
Though they've 'ad us out by marches an' they've
    'ad us back by rail;
But it runs as fast as troop-trains, and we cannot
    get away;
An' the sick-list to the Colonel makes ten more
    to-day.   15

There ain't no fun in women nor there ain't no
    bite to drink;

7 **bushed an' stoned** buried under a thornbush and covered with stones to prevent jackals or other wild animals from getting to the body

It's much too wet for shootin', we can only march
    and think;
An' at evenin', down the *nullahs*,° we can 'ear the
    jackals say,
"Get up, you rotten beggars, you've ten more
    to-day!"

'Twould make a monkey cough to see our way o'
    doin' things—   *20*
Lieutenants takin' companies an' captains takin'
    wings,
An' Lances actin' Sergeants—eight file to obey—
For we've lots o' quick promotion on ten deaths
    a day!

Our Colonel's white an' twitterly—'e gets no sleep
    nor food,
But mucks about in 'orspital where nothing does
    no good.   *25*
'E sends us 'eaps o' comforts, all bought from 'is
    pay—
But there aren't much comfort 'andy on ten
    deaths a day.

Our Chaplain's got a banjo, an' a skinny mule
    'e rides,
An' the stuff 'e says an' sings us, Lord, it makes
    us split our sides!
With 'is black coat-tails a-bobbin' to *Ta-ra-ra
    Boom-der-ay!*°   *30*
'E's the proper kind o' *padre* for ten deaths a day.

An' Father Victor 'elps 'im with our Roman
    Catholicks—

18 *nullahs* water holes (Hindustani) 30 *Ta-ra-ra Boom-der-ay* the refrain of a well-known music hall song. Kipling skillfully evokes the forced cheerfulness of the regimental priest.

He knows an 'eap of Irish songs an' rummy
 conjurin' tricks;
An' the two they works together when it comes
 to play or pray;
So we keep the ball a-rollin' on ten deaths a day. 35

We've got the cholerer in camp—we've got it 'ot
 an' sweet;
It ain't no Christmas dinner, but it's 'elped an' we
 must eat.
We've gone beyond the funkin', 'cause we've
 found it doesn't pay,
An' we're rockin' round the Districk on ten deaths
 a day!

 Then strike your camp an' go, the Rains are
  fallin',   40
  The Bugle's callin'!
 The dead are bushed an' stoned to keep 'em
  safe below!
 An' them that do not like it they can lump it,
 An' them that cannot stand it they can
  jump it;
 We've got to die somewhere—some way—
  some'ow—   45
 We might as well begin to do it now!
 Then, Number One, let down the tent-pole
  slow,
 Knock out the pegs an' 'old the corners—so!
 Fold in the flies, furl up the ropes, an' stow!
 Oh, strike—oh, strike your camp an' go! 50
  (Gawd 'elp us!)

      —*First published in* The Seven Seas
      (London and New York, 1896)

The Ladies

In the spirit of "Mandalay," this is a soldier's happy recollection of the fun he has had with different types of women. Kipling originally wrote the last verse as an epigraph to his short story "The Courting of Dinah Shadd" in 1890; it offers a populist, even democratic twist: that social class has no bearing since all women are the same "under their skins."

I've taken my fun where I've found it;
    I've rogued an' I've ranged in my time;
I've 'ad my pickin' o' sweet'earts,
    An' four o' the lot was prime.
One was an 'arf-caste widow,   5
    One was a woman at Prome,
One was the wife of a *jemadar-sais*,°
    An' one is a girl at 'ome.

Now I aren't no 'and with the ladies,
    For, takin' 'em all along,   10
You never can say till you've tried 'em,
    An' then you are like to be wrong.
There's times when you'll think that you
      mightn't,
    There's times when you'll know that you
      might;
But the things you will learn from the Yellow
    an' Brown,   15
    They'll 'elp you a lot with the White!

I was a young un at 'Oogli,°
    Shy as a girl to begin;
Aggie de Castrer she made me,
    An' Aggie was clever as sin;   20
Older than me, but my first un—

7 **jemadar-sais** head groom   17 **'Oogli** Hooghly, a town in the Calcutta hinterland named after its great river

More like a mother she were—
Showed me the way to promotion an' pay,
    An' I learned about women from 'er!

Then I was ordered to Burma,   25
    Actin' in charge o' Bazar,
An' I got me a tiddy° live 'eathen
    Through buyin' supplies off 'er pa.
Funny an' yellow an' faithful—
    Doll in a teacup she were,   30
But we lived on the square, like a true-married
    pair,
    An' I learned about women from 'er!

Then we was shifted to Neemuch°
    (Or I might ha' been keepin' 'er now),
An' I took with a shiny she-devil,   35
    The wife of a nigger at Mhow;°
'Taught me the gipsy-folks' *bolee*°
    Kind o' volcano she were,
For she knifed me one night 'cause I wished she
    was white,
    And I learned about women from 'er!   40

Then I come 'ome in the trooper,
    'Long of a kid o' sixteen—
Girl from a convent at Meerut,°
    The straightest I ever 'ave seen.
Love at first sight was 'er trouble,   45
    She didn't know what it were;
An' I wouldn't do such, 'cause I liked 'er too
    much,
    But—I learned about women from 'er!

27 **tiddy** little (from baby talk)   33 **Neemuch** Nimach, a town
in Madya Pradesh, India, close to the Rajasthan border, which
was a British fort   36 **Mhow** town in Madya Pradesh,
India   37 *bolee* slang   43 **Meerut** town in northwest India,
near Delhi

I've taken my fun where I've found it,
    An' now I must pay for my fun,   *50*
For the more you 'ave known o' the others
    The less will you settle to one;
An' the end of it's sittin' and thinkin',
    An' dreamin' Hell-fires to see;
So be warned by my lot (which I know you will
        not),   *55*
    An' learn about women from me!

    What did the Colonel's Lady think?
        Nobody never knew.
    Somebody asked the Sergeant's wife,
        An' she told 'em true!   *60*
    When you get to a man in the case,
        They're like as a row of pins—
    For the Colonel's Lady an' Judy O'Grady°
        Are sisters under their skins!

        —*First published in* The Seven Seas
        (London and New York, 1896)

---

63 **Judy O'Grady** used as a generic name for the wife of a
man in the ranks

Bill 'Awkins

One of Kipling's lesser efforts, this poem is based on a popular music hall song.

" 'As anybody seen Bill 'Awkins?"
    "Now 'ow in the devil would I know?"
" 'E's taken my girl out walkin',
    An' I've got to tell 'im so—
        Gawd—bless—'im!   5
    I've got to tell 'im so."

"D'yer know what 'e's like, Bill 'Awkins?"
    "Now what in the devil would I care?"
" 'E's the livin', breathin' image of an organ-
        grinder's monkey,
    With a pound of grease in 'is 'air—   10
        Gawd—bless—'im!
    An' a pound o' grease in 'is 'air."

"An' s'pose you met Bill 'Awkins,
    Now what in the devil 'ud ye do?"
"I'd open 'is cheek to 'is chin-strap buckle,   15
    An' bung up° 'is both eyes, too—
        Gawd—bless—'im!
    An' bung up 'is both eyes, too!"

"Look 'ere, where 'e comes, Bill 'Awkins!
    Now what in the devil will you say?"   20
"It isn't fit an' proper to be fightin' on a Sunday,
    So I'll pass 'im the time o' day—
        Gawd—bless—'im!
    I'll pass 'im the time o' day!"

—First published in Pall Mall Gazette *(2 May 1895)*

16 **bung up** close

The Mother-Lodge

*Less a Barrack-Room Ballad than an evocation of
Kipling's own pride and pleasure at having been a
member of the Masonic Lodge "Hope & Perseverance,
782 E.C." when he was living in Lahore. As he often
noted, he liked the lodge's multicultural, multiethnic basis.
This poem is one of several that give the lie to a
commonly held idea that Kipling was racially prejudiced.*

There was Rundle, Station Master,
    An' Beazeley of the Rail,
An' 'Ackman, Commissariat,°
    An' Donkin' o' the Jail;
An' Blake, Conductor-Sargent,   5
    Our Master twice was 'e,
With 'im that kept the Europe-shop,°
    Old Framjee Eduljee.

Outside—"Sergeant! Sir! Salute! Salaam!"
Inside—"Brother," an' it doesn't do no 'arm.   10
We met upon the Level an' we parted on the
    Square,
An' I was Junior Deacon in my Mother-Lodge
    out there!

We'd Bola Nath, Accountant,
    An' Saul the Aden Jew,
An' Din Mohammed, draughtsman   15
    Of the Survey Office too;
There was Babu Chuckerbutty,
    An' Amir Singh the Sikh,
An' Castro from the fittin'-sheds,
    The Roman Catholick!   20

We 'adn't good regalia,
    An' our Lodge was old an' bare,

3 **Commissariat** the section of the army responsible for serving
food, often in the form of a shop or cafeteria   7 **Europe-shop**
shop selling imported goods

84

But we knew the Ancient Landmarks,°
    An' we kep' 'em to a hair;
An' lookin' on it backwards   *25*
    It often strikes me thus,
There ain't such things as infidels,
    Excep', per'aps, it's us.

For monthly, after Labour,°
    We'd all sit down and smoke   *30*
(We dursn't give no banquits,
    Lest a Brother's caste were broke),
An' man on man got talkin'
    Religion an' the rest,
An' every man comparin'   *35*
    Of the God 'e knew the best.

So man on man got talkin',
    An' not a Brother stirred
Till mornin' waked the parrots
    An' that dam' brain-fever-bird;   *40*
We'd say 'twas 'ighly curious,
    An' we'd all ride 'ome to bed,
With Mo'ammed, God, an' Shiva
    Changin' pickets in our 'ead.

Full oft on Guv'ment service   *45*
    This rovin' foot 'ath pressed,
An' bore fraternal greetin's
    To the Lodges east an' west,
Accordin' as commanded
    From Kohat° to Singapore,   *50*
But I wish that I might see them
    In my Mother-Lodge once more!

I wish that I might see them,
    My Brethren black an' brown,

23 **knew the Ancient Landmarks** knew the old principles of the Freemasons   29 **after Labour** after the solemn rituals of a (Freemason's) lodge   50 **Kohat** town (and district) south of Peshawar, in the northwest of what is now Pakistan

With the trichies° smellin' pleasant   55
 An' the *hog-darn°* passin' down;
An' the old khansamah° snorin'
 On the bottle-khana° floor,
Like a Master in good standing
 With my Mother-Lodge once more!   60

Outside—"Sergeant! Sir! Salute! Salaam!"
Inside—"Brother," an' it doesn't do no 'arm.
We met upon the Level an' we parted on the
 Square,
An' I was Junior Deacon in my Mother-Lodge
 out there!

—First published in Pall Mall Gazette *(2 May 1895)*

---

55 **trichies** cheap cheroots made in Tiruchirappalli (formerly
Trichinopoly) in Tamil Nadu in southern India 56 *hog-darn*
cigar lighter 57 **khansamah** butler 58 **bottle-khana** pantry

"Follow Me 'Ome"

*In this poem—sometimes maudlin, sometimes more
upbeat—a soldier reflects on a dead comrade and—as
so often in such situations—wishes he had been a better
friend when he had the chance. The refrain and final
chorus recall the rituals of a military funeral.*

There was no one like 'im, 'Orse or Foot,
    Nor any o' the Guns I knew;
An' because it was so, why, o' course 'e went
        an' died,
    Which is just what the best men do.

So it's knock out your pipes an' follow me!   5
An' it's finish up your swipes° an' follow me!
    Oh, 'ark to the big drum callin',
        Follow me—follow me 'ome!

'Is mare she neighs the 'ole day long,
    She paws the 'ole night through,   10
An' she won't take 'er feed 'cause o' waitin' for
        'is step,
    Which is just what a beast would do.

'Is girl she goes with a bombardier
    Before 'er month is through;
An' the banns are up in church, for she's got the
        beggar hooked,   15
    Which is just what a girl would do.

We fought 'bout a dog—last week it were—
    No more than a round or two;
But I strook 'im cruel 'ard, an' I wish I 'adn't now,
    Which is just what a man can't do.   20

'E was all that I 'ad in the way of a friend,
    An' I've 'ad to find one new;

6 **swipes** weak beer

87

But I'd give my pay an' stripe for to get the
     beggar back,
    Which it's just too late to do.

So it's knock out your pipes an' follow me!   *25*
An' it's finish off your swipes an' follow me!
    Oh, 'ark to the fifes a-crawlin'!
    Follow me—follow me 'ome!

    Take 'im away! 'E's gone where the best
       men go.
    Take 'im away! An' the gun-wheels
       turnin' slow.   *30*
    Take 'im away! There's more from the
       place 'e come.
    Take 'im away, with the limber an' the
       drum.

For it's "Three rounds blank" an' follow me,
An' it's "Thirteen rank" an' follow me;
    Oh, passin' the love o' women,   *35*
    Follow me—follow me 'ome!

—*First published in* Pall Mall Magazine *(June 1894)*

The Sergeant's Weddin'

A good-natured ballad about the wedding of a roguish sergeant. Kipling self-censored his text, for he originally had the sergeant marrying "a 'ore" and later changed it to "etc." (though of course his readers could guess the missing word by the rhyme scheme). The poem is nevertheless far from coy about the sergeant's dishonesty in shortchanging his customers at the canteen, allowing him to buy himself a buggy.

'E was warned agin' 'er—
    That's what made 'im look;
She was warned agin' 'im—
    That is why she took.
'Wouldn't 'ear no reason,   5
    'Went an' done it blind;
We know all about 'em,
    They've got all to find!

    Cheer for the Sergeant's weddin'—
        Give 'em one cheer more!   10
    Grey gun-'orses in the lando,
        An' a rogue is married to, etc.

What's the use o' tellin'
    'Arf the lot she's been?
'E's a bloomin' robber,   15
    An' 'e keeps canteen.
'Ow did 'e get 'is buggy?
    Gawd, you needn't ask!
'Made 'is forty gallon
    Out of every cask!   20

Watch 'im, with 'is 'air cut,
    Count us filin' by—
Won't the Colonel praise 'is
    Pop—u—lar—i—ty!
We 'ave scores to settle—   25

Scores for more than beer;
She's the girl to pay 'em—
    That is why we're 'ere!

See the chaplain thinkin'?
    See the women smile?   30
Twig the married winkin'
    As they take the aisle?
Keep your side-arms quiet,
    Dressin' by the Band.
Ho! You 'oly beggars,   35
    Cough be'ind your 'and!

Now it's done an' over,
    'Ear the organ squeak,
"*Voice that breathed o'er Eden*"—°
    Ain't she got the cheek!   40
White an' laylock ribbons,
    Think yourself so fine!
I'd pray Gawd to take yer
    'Fore I made yer mine!

Escort to the kerridge,   45
    Wish 'im luck, the brute!
Chuck the slippers after—
    (Pity 'tain't a boot!)
Bowin' like a lady,
    Blushin' like a lad—   50
'Oo would say to see 'em
    Both is rotten bad?

Cheer for the Sergeant's weddin'—
    Give 'em one cheer more!
Grey gun-'orses in the lando,   55
    An' a rogue is married to, etc.

                —*First published in* The Seven Seas
                    (London and New York, 1896)

39 "*Voice that breathed o'er Eden*" first line of a wedding
hymn written in 1857 by John Keble (1792–1866)

The Jacket

*This ballad recalls an incident associated with Captain
J. Dalbiac during the 1882 war against Arabi Pasha in
Egypt. When an officer was promoted from the Field
Artillery to the more coveted Royal Horse Artillery, he
was allowed to wear a gold-laced jacket, which was called
colloquially "getting his jacket." Dalbiac, who was known
as a practical joker, celebrated his assumption of the
jacket by ferrying three dozen bottles of beer to his men
in a linder that should have been carrying ammunition.*

Through the Plagues of Egyp' we was chasin'
   Arabi,
 Gettin' down an' shovin' in the sun;
An' you might 'ave called us dirty, an' you might
   ha' called us dry,
 An' you might 'ave 'eard us talkin' at the gun.
But the Captain 'ad 'is jacket, an' the jacket it
   was new—   5
 ('Orse Gunners, listen to my song!)
An' the wettin' of the jacket is the proper thing
   to do,
 Nor we didn't keep 'im waitin' very long.

One day they gave us orders for to shell a sand
   redoubt,
 Loadin' down the axle-arms with case;   10
But the Captain knew 'is dooty, an' he took the
   crackers out
 An' he put some proper liquor in its place.
An' the Captain saw the shrapnel, which is six-
   an'-thirty clear.
 ('Orse Gunners, listen to my song!)
"Will you draw the weight," sez 'e, "or will you
   draw the beer?"   15
 An' we didn't keep 'im waitin' very long.
  For the Captain, etc.

91

Then we trotted gentle, not to break the
   bloomin' glass,
  Though the Arabites 'ad all their ranges
   marked;
But we dursn't 'ardly gallop, for the most was
   bottled Bass,   *20*
  An' we'd dreamed of it since we was
   disembarked:
So we fired economic with the shells we 'ad in
   'and,
  ('Orse Gunners, listen to my song!)
But the beggars under cover 'ad the impidence
   to stand,
  An' we couldn't keep 'em waitin' very long. *25*
   And the Captain, etc.

So we finished 'arf the liquor (an' the Captain
   took champagne),
  An' the Arabites was shootin' all the while;
An' we left our wounded 'appy with the empties
   on the plain,
  An' we used the bloomin' guns for pro-jec-tile! *30*
We limbered up an' galloped—there were nothin'
   else to do—
  ('Orse Gunners, listen to my song!)
An' the Battery came a-boundin' like a boundin'
   kangaroo,
  But they didn't watch us comin' very long.
   As the Captain, etc.   *35*

We was goin' most extended—we was drivin'
   very fine,
  An' the Arabites were loosin' 'igh an' wide,
Till the Captain took the glassy with a rattlin'
   right incline,
  An' we dropped upon their 'eads the other
   side.
Then we give 'em quarter—such as 'adn't up
   and cut,   *40*

The Jacket

('Orse Gunners, listen to my song!)
An' the Captain stood a limberful of fizzy—
    somethin' Brutt,
    But we didn't leave it fizzing very long.
       For the Captain, etc.

We might ha' been court-martialled, but it all
    come out all right   45
    When they signalled us to join the main
    command.
There was every round expended, there was every
    gunner tight,
    An' the Captain waved a corkscrew in 'is 'and.
       But the Captain 'ad 'is jacket, etc.

—First published in The Seven Seas
(London and New York, 1896)

The 'Eathen

This ballad is about the gradual regimentation of a young recruit—how he starts out not knowing anything and gradually ascends through the noncommissioned ranks as he absorbs his training.

The 'eathen in 'is blindness° bows down to wood
      an' stone;
'E don't obey no orders unless they is 'is own;
'E keeps 'is side-arms awful: 'e leaves 'em all
      about,
An' then comes up the regiment an' pokes the
      'eathen out.

    All along o' dirtiness, all along o' mess,   5
    All along o' doin' things rather-more-or-less,
    All along of abby-nay,° kul,° an' hazar-ho,°
    Mind you keep your rifle an' yourself jus' so!

The young recruit is 'aughty—'e draf's from Gawd
      knows where;
They bid 'im show 'is stockin's an' lay 'is
      mattress square;   10
'E calls it bloomin' nonsense—'e doesn't know
      no more—
An' then up comes 'is Company an' kicks 'im
      round the floor!

The young recruit is 'ammered—'e takes it very
      'ard;
'E 'angs 'is 'ead an' mutters—'e sulks about the
      yard;
'E talks o' "cruel tyrants" 'e'll swing for by-an'-by,   15

1 **The 'eathen in 'is blindness** recalls lines from the hymn "From Greenland's Icy Mountains" written in 1819 by Bishop Reginald Heber (1783–1826) 7 **abby-nay** not now **kul** tomorrow **hazar-ho** wait a bit

An' the others 'ears an' mocks 'im, an' the boy
    goes orf to cry.

The young recruit is silly—'e thinks o' suicide;
'E's lost 'is gutter-devil;° 'e 'asn't got 'is pride;
But day by day they kicks 'im, which 'elps 'im on
    a bit,
Till 'e finds 'isself one mornin' with a full an'
    proper kit.   *20*

    Gettin' clear o' dirtiness, gettin' done with
        mess,
    Gettin' shut o' doin' things rather-more-or-
        less;
    Not so fond of abby-nay, kul, nor hazar-ho,
    Learns to keep 'is rifle an' 'isself jus' so!

The young recruit is 'appy—'e throws a chest to
    suit;   *25*
You see 'im grow mustaches; you 'ear 'im slap
    'is boot;
'E learns to drop the "bloodies" from every word
    'e slings,
An' 'e shows an 'ealthy brisket° when 'e strips for
    bars an' rings.

The cruel-tyrant-sergeants they watch 'im 'arf a
    year;
They watch 'im with 'is comrades, they watch 'im
    with 'is beer;   *30*
They watch 'im with the women at the
    regimental dance,
And the cruel-tyrant-sergeants send 'is name
    along for "Lance."

An' now 'e's 'arf o' nothin', an' all a private yet,
'Is room they up an' rags 'im to see what they
    will get;

18 **gutter-devil** street cunning   28 **brisket** chest

They rags 'im low an' cunnin', each dirty trick
       they can,   35
But 'e learns to sweat 'is temper° an' 'e learns to
       sweat 'is man.°

An', last, a Colour-Sergeant, as such to be obeyed,
'E schools 'is men at cricket, 'e tells 'em on
           parade;
They sees 'em quick an' 'andy, uncommon set
           an' smart,
An' so 'e talks to orficers which 'ave the Core
       at 'eart.   40

'E learns to do 'is watchin' without it showin'
           plain;
'E learns to save a dummy, an' shove 'im
           straight again;
'E learns to check a ranker that's buyin' leave
       to shirk;
An' 'e learns to make men like 'im so they'll learn
       to like their work.

An' when it comes to marchin' he'll see their
           socks are right,   45
An' when it comes to action 'e shows 'em 'ow
       to sight;
'E knows their ways of thinkin' and just what's in
       their mind;
'E knows when they are takin' on an' when
       they've fell be'ind.

'E knows each talkin' corpril that leads a squad
           astray;
'E feels 'is innards 'eavin', 'is bowels givin' way;   50
'E sees the blue-white faces all tryin' 'ard to grin,

36 **sweat 'is temper** keep his temper **sweat 'is man** make the
other guy sweat

An' 'e stands an' waits an' suffers till it's time to
      cap 'em in.°

An' now the hugly bullets come peckin' through
      the dust,
An' no one wants to face 'em, but every beggar
      must;
So, like a man in irons which isn't glad to go,   *55*
They moves 'em off by companies uncommon stiff
      an' slow.

Of all 'is five years' schoolin' they don't
      remember much
Excep' the not retreatin', the step an' keepin'
      touch.
It looks like teachin' wasted when they duck an'
      spread an' 'op,
But if 'e 'adn't learned 'em they'd be all about
      the shop!   *60*

An' now it's " 'Oo goes backward?" an' now it's
      " 'Oo comes on?"
And now it's "Get the doolies,"° an' now the
      captain's gone;
An' now it's bloody murder, but all the while
      they 'ear
'Is voice, the same as barrick drill, a-shepherdin'
      the rear.

'E's just as sick as they are, 'is 'eart is like to split,   *65*
But 'e works 'em, works 'em, works 'em till he
      feels 'em take the bit;
The rest is 'oldin' steady till the watchful bugles
      play,

52 **cap 'em in** bring them in (from fox hunting, in which the
huntsman waves his cap to encourage the hounds into a covert).
Kipling's meaning here is ambiguous: are the soldiers being
brought into barracks or into line for fighting? 62 **doolies**
stretchers

An' 'e lifts 'em, lifts 'em, lifts 'em through the
  charge that wins the day!

The 'eathen in 'is blindness bows down to wood
  an' stone;
'E don't obey no orders unless they is 'is own;   70
The 'eathen in 'is blindness must end where 'e
  began,
But the backbone of the Army is the non-
  commissioned man!

 Keep away from dirtiness—keep away from
   mess.
 Don't get into doin' things rather-more-or-less!
 Let's ha' done with abby-nay, kul, an' hazar-ho;   75
 Mind you keep your rifle an' yourself jus' so!

   —*First published in* McClure's Magazine
      (September 1896)

The Shut-Eye Sentry

One of the duties of an orderly officer in the barracks was to do the "rounds"—visiting the sentries and turning out the guard. But in this jovial ballad the officer is blind drunk and can't even stand up without the help of his noncommissioned officers.

Sez the Junior Orderly Sergeant
    To the Senior Orderly Man:
"Our Orderly Orf'cer's *hokee-mut*,°
    You 'elp 'im all you can.
For the wine was old and the night is cold,   5
    An' the best we may go wrong,
So, 'fore 'e gits to the sentry-box,
    You pass the word along."

  So it was "Rounds! What Rounds?" at two of
      a frosty night,
    'E's 'oldin' on by the sergeant's sash, but,
      sentry, shut your eye.   10
  An' it was "Pass! All's well!" Oh, ain't 'e
      drippin' tight!
    'E'll need an affidavit pretty badly by-an'-by.

The moon was white on the barricks,
    The road was white an' wide,
An' the Orderly Orf'cer took it all,   15
    An' the ten-foot ditch beside.
An' the corporal pulled an' the sergeant pushed,
    An' the three they danced along,
But I'd shut my eyes in the sentry-box,
    So I didn't see nothin' wrong.   20

  Though it was "Rounds! What Rounds?" O
      corporal, 'old 'im up!

3 *hokee-mut* blind drunk (with the added connotation of being sick)

99

'E's usin' 'is cap as it shouldn't be used,
    but, sentry, shut your eye.
An' it was "Pass! All's well!" Ho, shun the
        foamin' cup!
    'E'll need, etc.

'Twas after four in the mornin';   25
    We 'ad to stop the fun,
An' we sent 'im 'ome on a bullock-cart,
    With 'is belt an' stock undone;
But we sluiced 'im down an' we washed 'im out,
    An' a first-class job we made,   30
When we saved 'im, smart as a bombardier,
    For six-o'clock parade.

It 'ad been "Rounds! What Rounds?" Oh,
        shove 'im straight again!
    'E's usin' 'is sword for a bicycle, but, sentry,
        shut your eye.
An' it was "Pass! All's well!" 'E's called me
        "Darlin' Jane"!   35
    'E'll need, etc.

The drill was long an' 'eavy,
    The sky was 'ot an' blue,
An' 'is eye was wild an' 'is 'air was wet,
    But 'is sergeant pulled 'im through.   40
Our men was good old trusties—
    They'd done it on their 'ead;
But you ought to 'ave 'eard 'em markin' time
    To 'ide the things 'e said!

For it was "Right flank—wheel!" for " 'Alt, an'
        stand at ease!"   45
    An' "Left extend!" for "Centre close!" O
        marker, shut your eye!
An' it was, " 'Ere, sir, 'ere! before the Colonel
        sees!"

So he needed affidavits pretty badly by-
an'-by.

There was two-an'-thirty sergeants,
  There was corp'rals forty-one,   50
There was just nine 'undred rank an' file
  To swear to a touch o' sun.
There was me 'e'd kissed in the sentry-box,
  As I 'ave not told in my song,
But I took my oath, which were Bible truth,   55
  I 'adn't seen nothin' wrong.

There's them that's 'ot an' 'aughty,
  There's them that's cold an' 'ard,
But there comes a night when the best gets tight,
  And then turns out the Guard.   60
I've seen them 'ide their liquor
  In every kind o' way,
But most depends on makin' friends
  With Privit Thomas A.!

When it is "Rounds! What Rounds?" 'E's
    breathin' through 'is nose.   65
  'E's reelin', rollin', roarin' tight, but, sentry,
    shut your eye.
An' it is "Pass! All's well!" An' that's the way
    it goes:
  We'll 'elp 'im for 'is mother, an' 'e'll 'elp
    us by-an'-by!

—*First published in* The Seven Seas
(London and New York, 1896)

"Mary, Pity Women!"

Anyone who doubts Kipling's sympathy for the female sex should study this heartfelt ballad about a woman who has been made pregnant by an impoverished soldier who refuses to marry her ("I want the name— no more").

In his posthumous autobiography, Something of Myself *(1937), Kipling said that the ballad was suggested to him by a barmaid he used to talk to at Gatti's Music Hall, close to the apartment he rented in Villiers Street when he first came to London in 1889.*

You call yourself a man,
    For all you used to swear,
An' leave me, as you can,
    My certain shame to bear?
I 'ear! You do not care—   5
    You done the worst you know.
I 'ate you, grinnin' there. . . .
    Ah, Gawd, I love you so!

Nice while it lasted, an' now it is over—
Tear out your 'eart an' good-bye to your lover!   10
What's the use o' grievin', when the mother that
    bore you
(Mary, pity women!) knew it all before you?

It aren't no false alarm,
    The finish to your fun;
You—you 'ave brung the 'arm,   15
    An' I'm the ruined one;
An' now you'll off an' run
    With some new fool in tow.
Your 'eart? You 'aven't none. . . .
    Ah, Gawd, I love you so!   20

When a man is tired there is naught will bind 'im;
All 'e solemn promised 'e will shove be'ind 'im.

What's the good o' prayin' for The Wrath to
  strike 'im
(Mary, pity women!), when the rest are like
  'im?

What 'ope for me or—it?   25
    What's left for us to do?
I've walked with men a bit,
    But this—but this is you.
So 'elp me Christ, it's true!
    Where can I 'ide or go?   30
You coward through and through! . . .
    Ah, Gawd, I love you so!

All the more you give 'em the less are they
    for givin'—
Love lies dead, an' you cannot kiss 'im livin'.
Down the road 'e led you there is no returnin'   35
(Mary, pity women!), but you're late in learnin'!

You'd like to treat me fair?
    You can't, because we're pore?
We'd starve? What do I care!
    We might, but *this* is shore!   40
I want the name—no more—
    The name, an' lines to show,
An' not to be an 'ore. . . .
    Ah, Gawd, I love you so!

What's the good o' pleadin', when the mother
    that bore you   45
(Mary, pity women!) knew it all before you?
Sleep on 'is promises an' wake to your sorrow
(Mary, pity women!), for we sail to-morrow!

—First published in Pall Mall Magazine
(February 1894)

For to Admire

An underappreciated example of Kipling's genius for capturing both the happiness and the sadness locked in a soldier's memory.

The Injian Ocean sets an' smiles
    So sof', so bright, so bloomin' blue;
There aren't a wave for miles an' miles
    Excep' the jiggle from the screw.°
The ship is swep', the day is done,   5
    The bugle's gone for smoke and play;
An' black agin' the settin' sun
    The Lascar° sings, "*Hum deckty hai!*"°

    For to admire an' for to see,
        For to be'old this world so wide—   10
    It never done no good to me,
        But I can't drop it if I tried!

I see the sergeants pitchin' quoits,
    I 'ear the women laugh an' talk,
I spy upon the quarter-deck   15
    The orficers an' lydies walk.
I thinks about the things that was,
    An' leans an' looks acrost the sea,
Till spite of all the crowded ship
    There's no one lef' alive but me.   20

The things that was which I 'ave seen,
    In barrick, camp, an' action too,
I tells them over by myself,
    An' sometimes wonders if they're true;
For they was odd—most awful odd—   25
    But all the same now they are o'er,
There must be 'eaps o' plenty such,
    An' if I wait I'll see some more.

4 **screw** propeller 8 **Lascar** Indian seaman *"Hum deckty hai"* I'm looking out.

104

Oh, I 'ave come upon the books,°
    An' frequent broke a barrick rule,   30
An' stood beside an' watched myself
    Be'avin' like a bloomin' fool.
I paid my price for findin' out,
    Nor never grutched the price I paid,
But sat in Clink without my boots,   35
    Admirin' 'ow the world was made.

Be'old a crowd upon the beam,
    An' 'umped above the sea appears
Old Aden,° like a barrick-stove
    That no one's lit for years an' years!   40
I passed by that when I began,
    An' I go 'ome the road I came,
A time-expired soldier-man
    With six years' service to 'is name.

My girl she said, "Oh, stay with me!"   45
    My mother 'eld me to 'er breast.
They've never written none, an' so
    They must 'ave gone with all the rest—
With all the rest which I 'ave seen
    An' found an' known an' met along.   50
I cannot say the things I feel,
    And so I sing my evenin' song:

    For to admire an' for to see,
        For to be'old this world so wide—
    It never done no good to me,   55
        But I can't drop it if I tried!

—*First published in* Pall Mall Gazette
(February 1894)

29 **come upon the books** been named in the register of bad
conduct   39 **Aden** This port town in Yemen, in southern
Arabia, was an important stopping place on the voyage
between Europe and India.

L'envoi

Not strictly a Barrack-Room Ballad, this short piece draws the poems to a close. Adopting a tone that is slightly too reminiscent of Victorian hymn writers, it looks to a happy afterlife, when everyone is able to work at the thing he or she loves.

When Earth's last picture is painted and the tubes
    are twisted and dried,
When the oldest colours have faded, and the
    youngest critic has died,
We shall rest, and, faith, we shall need it—lie
    down for an aeon or two,
Till the Master of All Good Workmen shall put
    us to work anew!

And those that were good shall be happy: they
    shall sit in a golden chair;   5
They shall splash at a ten-league canvas with
    brushes of comets' hair;
They shall find real saints to draw from—
    Magdalene, Peter, and Paul;
They shall work for an age at a sitting and never
    be tired at all!

And only the Master shall praise us, and only the
    Master shall blame;
And no one shall work for money, and no one
    shall work for fame,   10
But each for the joy of the working, and each, in
    his separate star,
Shall draw the Thing as he sees It for the God of
    Things as They Are!

—*First published in* The New York Sun *(15 May 1892)*

106

Selected Bibliography

Other Works by Rudyard Kipling

Departmental Ditties, 1886 Poems
Plain Tales from the Hills, 1888 Stories
Soldiers Three, 1888 Stories
Wee Willie Winkie and Other Stories, 1889 Stories
The Light That Failed, 1890 Novel
Life's Handicap, 1891 Stories
Many Inventions, 1893 Stories
The Jungle Book, 1894 Stories (Signet Classic)
The Second Jungle Book, 1895 Stories
The Seven Seas, 1896 Poems
Captains Courageous, 1897 Novel (Signet Classic)
The Day's Work, 1898 Stories
Stalky & Co., 1899 Novel
Kim, 1901 Novel
Just So Stories, 1902 Stories
The Five Nations, 1903 Poems
Traffics and Discoveries, 1904 Stories
Puck of Pook's Hill, 1906 Stories
Actions and Reactions, 1909 Stories

Rewards and Fairies, 1910 Stories

A Diversity of Creatures, 1917 Stories

The Years Between, 1919 Poems

Debits and Credits, 1926 Stories

Limits and Renewals, 1932 Stories

Something of Myself, 1937 Autobiography

Biography and Criticism

Amis, Kingsley. *Rudyard Kipling and His World.* New York: Scribners, 1975.

Bauer, Helen Pike. *Rudyard Kipling: A Study of the Short Fiction.* New York: Twayne, 1994.

Bloom, Harold, ed. *Rudyard Kipling.* Modern Critical Views. New York: Chelsea House, 1987.

Carrington, Charles E. *Rudyard Kipling: His Life and Works.* Rev. ed. London: Macmillan, 1978.

Dobree, Bonamy. *Rudyard Kipling, Realist and Fabulist.* London: Oxford University Press, 1967.

Eliot, T. S. *A Choice of Kipling's Verse, Made by T. S. Eliot, with an Essay on Rudyard Kipling.* London: Faber and Faber, 1941.

Gilbert, E. L., ed. *Kipling and the Critics.* New York: New York University Press, 1965.

Green, Roger Lancelyn. *Kipling: The Critical Heritage.* London: Routledge and Kegan Paul, 1971.

Gross, John, ed. *The Age of Kipling.* New York: Simon & Schuster, 1972.

Harrison, James. *Rudyard Kipling.* Boston: Twayne, 1982.

Kipling, Rudyard. *Rudyard Kipling: Something of Myself and Other Autobiographical Writings.* Ed. Thomas Pinney. Cambridge: Cambridge University Press, 1990.

Selected Bibliography

Lycett, Andrew. *Rudyard Kipling.* London: Weidenfeld and Nicolson, 1999.

Orel, Harold, ed. *Critical Essays on Rudyard Kipling.* Boston: G. K. Hall, 1989.

Page, Norman. *A Kipling Companion.* London: Macmillan, 1984.

Ricketts, Harry. *Rudyard Kipling: A Life.* New York: Carroll and Graf, 2000.

Seymour-Smith, Martin. *Rudyard Kipling.* New York: St. Martin's, 1990.

Sullivan, Zohreh T. *Narratives of Empire: The Fictions of Rudyard Kipling.* New York: Cambridge University Press, 1993.

Wilson, Angus. *The Strange Ride of Rudyard Kipling: His Life and Works.* New York: Viking, 1977.

READ THE TOP 25 SIGNET CLASSICS

Animal Farm by George Orwell — 0-451-52634-1

1984 by George Orwell — 0-451-52493-4

Hamlet by William Shakespeare — 0-451-52692-9

Frankenstein by Mary Shelley — 0-451-52771-2

The Scarlet Letter by Nathaniel Hawthorne — 0-451-52608-2

The Adventures of Huckleberry Finn by Mark Twain — 0-451-52650-3

The Odyssey by Homer — 0-451-52736-4

Frankenstein, Dracula, Dr. Jekyll and Mr. Hyde

by Mary Shelley, Bram Stoker, and Robert Louis Stevenson

— 0-451-52363-6

Jane Eyre by Charlotte Bronte — 0-451-52655-4

Heart of Darkness & The Secret Sharer
by Joseph Conrad — 0-451-52657-0

Great Expectations by Charles Dickens — 0-451-52671-6

Beowulf (Burton Raffel, translator) — 0-451-52740-2

Ethan Frome by Edith Wharton — 0-451-52766-6

Narrative of the Life of Frederick Douglass
by Frederick Douglass — 0-451-52673-2

A Tale of Two Cities by Charles Dickens — 0-451-52656-2

Othello by William Shakespeare — 0-451-52685-6

One Day in the Life of Ivan Denisovich

by Alexander Solzhenitsyn — 0-451-52709-7

Pride and Prejudice by Jane Austen — 0-451-52588-4

Uncle Tom's Cabin: 150th Anniversary Edition — 0-451-52670-8

Macbeth by William Shakespeare — 0-451-52677-5

The Count of Monte Cristo by Alexander Dumas — 0-451-52195-1

Romeo and Juliet by William Shakespeare — 0-451-52686-4

A Midsummer Night's Dream by William Shakespeare — 0-451-52696-1

The Prince — 0-451-52746-1

Wuthering Heights by Emily Bronte — 0-451-52338-5

To order call: 1-800-788-6262

 SIGNET CLASSIC (0451)

Classics of the **American Renaissance**

THE HOUSE OF THE SEVEN GABLES
by Nathaniel Hawthorne
(527917)
"God will give him blood to drink!" An evil house, cursed through the centuries by a man who was hanged for witchcraft, haunted by the ghosts of its sinful dead, wracked by the fear of its frightened living....

THE CELESTIAL RAILROAD & Other Stories
by Nathaniel Hawthorne
(522133)
Poignant, enlightening, funny and sometimes even frightening, this collection contains eighteen of Hawthorne's greatest stories, stories which provide a direct insight into the workings of the human soul.

MOBY DICK
by Herman Melville
(526996)
One of the greatest achievements of western literature, this book has it all; a ghost story, an encounter with a cannibal, travels to exotic lands—and the strange customs encountered there, and most of all—a thrilling chase on the high seas—and the final battle to the death between the crew of the tiny Pequod and the majestic, supernatural whale.

BILLY BUDD & Other Tales
by Herman Melville
(526872)
Collected here are Melville's greatest stories, wry and insightful, or tragic and moving; they contain some of the most vivid writing in the English language.

To order call: 1-800-788-6262